CHICAGO COPS APB

CHICAGO COPS APB

William L. Prentiss

Commonwealth Books Inc.,

A Commonwealth Publications Trade
CHICAGO COPS APB
This edition published 2022
by Commonwealth Books Inc.,
All rights reserved

Library of Congress Control Number: 2022938886

ISBN: 978-1-892986-34-4 (Trade)
ISBN: 978-1-892986-46-7 (E-PUB)

This work is a novel and any similarity to actual persons or events is purely coincidental.

First Commonwealth Books Trade Edition: June 2022

PUBLISHED BY COMMONWEALTH BOOKS, INC.,
www.commonwealthbooks@aol.com
www.commonwealthbooksinc.com

Manufactured in the United States of America

Prologue

Scenes of murder left detective Leo Carey in subdued rage, and this one also made him sick to his stomach. Upon hearing the news he put a hand over his face and murmured, "Aw no."

The life was snuffed out so brutally, and the victim so prominent, the news would cause mourning throughout Chicago. Even children for whom the sordid details of murder are rarely brought into their lives, would be made aware and suffer from this crime.

Leo's loathing for the spectacle of a life or lives being ended by the act of murder was replaced by hatred almost as soon as he arrived at the scene. It was a hatred for the act of murder, but especially for the person or persons who took this life.

1

It was rookie Leo Carey's last month on Patrol and Investigative Services when he decided what kind of cop he would be. He was riding shot gun on late night patrol with ten-year veteran Ted Serbo. As their blue and White cruised west on 55th between Lake Park and Cottage Grove a Black youth leaped from the sidewalk in front of their car waving his arms.

Serbo murmured , "Oops," and pulled hard right on the street packed with parked cars but little traffic. Leo had his door open while the car was still moving, He was in front of the kid in seconds and grabbed his arm.

"Take it easy, man. What's up?"

The kid, late teens, eyes bulging, yelled,

"Kathy's dead. Oh Jesus, Kathy's dead."

Serbo had called in their position and was alongside his partner. In the kid's face they chorused, "Where?"

The kid could have been high. It didn't matter. He jerked a skinny arm toward the alley alongside the tavern.

"In there."

"It was familiar territory to Leo. The alley lay alongside a bar called The Bear. His one-bedroom apartment was only a few blocks from the restaurant-bar in the heart of the University of Chicago district.

The kid ran into the dark. "Here," he yelled, "Here. Right here!"

But she wasn't right there. There was nothing in the dimly lit alley but a dumpster and a pair of over-filled garbage cans alongside empty cardboard beer cartons. The kid pointed at a spot alongside the dumpster.

"She was here. All woozy. Her eyes were shut. He was holding her up. Then she fell, right here."

Leo was in the kid's face, "Who's the guy?"

"Jeff. Jeffrey Blanchard. He's been trying to get in her pants all semester. He put something in her drink."

Serbo said, "Looks like a date rape gone wrong. Maybe she's ok. She might have walked out of here."

The kid's "No. No way" was drowned out by an engine revving at the dark end of the alley. No lights, but a foot had come down hard on the accelerator.

"That's him," the youth pointed into the dark. "That's his pickup."

A couple of hours later, Leo and Serbo put together a report that left heads shaking from the night desk right up to Superintendent Louis Mangano's office.

"Carey went bananas. He's lucky he wasn't killed," was the general agreement although no one questioned the young officer's courage.

Serbo later told a roomful of cops, "What Leo did was step in front of the vehicle. He's a cop. He held up his hands. The driver should stop. Right?

"Wrong. The truck was probably doing twenty when Leo decided the driver had gone nuts and was going to kill him. It's too late to jump clear. What he does is dive forward like he's going into a pool? Thank God the truck didn't have a hood ornament. It would have ripped off his balls. A second or two later Leo was over the cab and into the truck bed."

The report Leo and his partner submitted began somewhat differently although Serbo's informal version was basically correct.

The report they signed included what happened after Leo left his feet, but Serbo's unofficial version, free of formal police syntax, was more entertaining.

Leo told his granddad, Damon,

"I thought I was in big trouble when I flew over that cab. I saw the eyes of the kid driver while I was in the air. Crazy and scared out of his mind. What was he thinking? That he was going to get away? I landed on my belly, bounced over the cab and landed in the truck bed. Thank God the tail gate was up. The truck was out of the alley and turned toward Cottage. It just missed our car. I grabbed my thirty eight but what the hell. What could I do? The kid is now doing fifty with his foot on the gas. I crawled over a lump wrapped in something. Turned out to be the poor girl in a tarp.

"I rapped on the glass window, but the kid acted as if he didn't hear me. He was hunched over the wheel, at least looking where the hell he was going, when I smashed the glass. I stuck the gun against his head and yelled, "You can do time for manslaughter or you die right here. What's it going to be?" Thank God the kid had some sense left. He stopped the truck."

Serbo was waiting for him outside the un- versity hospital's emergency room, handcuffs ready. A gurney was ready and Leo walked alongside it into the blazing lights. He thought he would wait for a report on Kathy Schultz's condition, but he and Serbo were ordered to the station. He had to settle for an nurse's promise he would get a call.

He told Serbo, "I couldn't shoot the kid and try to grab the wheel. We were doing at least sixty. We both would've been killed."

Jeffrey Blanchard's also made the correct decision. His intelligence prevailed over his panic. The cop's hard gun against his head brought his mind into focus for the first time in the past few minutes.

He would call his lawyer father who would tell him to keep his mouth shut, admit nothing. He certainly didn't mean to harm Kathy. It was an accident and he would probably go to jail, but his wealthy parents would protect him. He panicked after she collapsed in his arms, at least unconscious. He thought only of escape. He had a tarp in the truck. He would wrap her body and dump her somewhere, then run, maybe Mexico.

His better sense took over. Who was he kidding? He had fifty bucks in his wallet. Using a credit cards would be an announcement, "Come and get me."

He pulled the pickup over to the curb, leaving both hands on the wheel as the cop scrambled out of the truck bed and into the cab

Fortunately, Kathy survived the date rape drug and rough handling. The would-be rapist would be punished, the extent to be determined, but he rejoiced with his parents that he had not committed murder.

The incident was surely helpful in Leo's shift into Investigative Services, detective division, assigned to violent crime. He became known as a tireless worker, cooperative, and possessed of an uncanny sense for choosing the right trail.

He told his friend, Tribune columnist Sid Coffin, "It isn't like TV or the movies. God, it can be hard work digging up the links, but once you think you have your man, or woman, it's almost fun to play it out."

As a young south-sider Leo decided he would be a Catholic priest, but on his fourteenth birthday while sharing a Sunday dinner with his grandfather, the young orphan said, "Granddad, I want to be a policeman, like you were."

Damon Carey wasn't too keen on the idea. He had survived forty years of service, a great deal of it on a south-side Chicago beat, but his son, Francis James, was dead after only three. Francis called Fran, was Leo's dad. He died in a three-car pileup chasing a car thief down Stoney Island Avenue. Damon felt no bitterness toward police work as a result of the tragedy, but the huge changes in law enforcement, especially for street cops, and the much greater danger since his day, made him hope his bright and active grandson might change his mind and seek another career.

"It's so different from my time, Leo. There's a lot more danger. The drugs are making zombies out of people and anyone can get a gun. A street cop doesn't have the respect we had, either."

He might have added that in his day officers didn't cover their beats behind a wheel. They walked several miles a day, or night, and were sometimes feared, even disliked, but usually respected by the general run of Chicagoans. Damon had never fired his standard issue thirty-eight while on duty, but his night stick was always a threat. The rule was to always maintain a tough exterior. It never occurred to Damon Carey to speak tactfully to anyone, Black or White, if they were threatening the peace.

Leo went ahead with his plan, did well in the academy, and with the backing of a couple of his late father's friends, he moved through the ranks, sideways at first, but gradually upwards, achieving the rank of Sergeant in the homicide division by the time he was thirty. He never wore a uniform again, except for special occasions. In a way, he reasoned, he would fulfill the career of his dad, Francis Carey, and help fill the void caused by the loss of his mother who was also a victim of her husband's early demise. Ann Carey never recovered from the loss of her husband. She began drinking heavily, and was dead at only thirty nine years from tuberculosis.

Granddad Damon and his wife, Nel, reared Leo who they proudly avowed was a good kid. Leo repaid their love and support by tending to business at St. Cyril's grammar school and Mount Carmel high where he earned part of his tuition as a tight end. He did two years in social studies at Wilson Junior college before beginning his career in law enforcement.

His grandfather began his service during the worst depression in U.S. history. He walked a beat during those years, ultimately retiring as a desk Sergeant in the Woodlawn district. During his entire career, he raised his night stick a half- dozen times, but never saw a gun held by any other person than a fellow cop.

He enjoyed telling Leo how enjoyed most of his days and nights as a cop.

"You know, we didn't have a CAPS (Chicago Alternative Policing Strategy) during my years on a beat. The goals of having squads of beat cops make friends with local residents and businesses and learning the general make up a community were things I did as a matter of course. I knew most of the neighborhood kids and their parents, and all of the shop owners along sixty third street. And I was on my own.

"Fortunately, it was a law abiding neighborhood. About the only problems were domestic disputes and rare house break ins. The only addiction was booze, and the drunks who made public nuisances of themselves got tossed in the tank. A night in a cell can be very sobering.

"I never broke a head with my stick. I once bounced it after a kid I saw trying to boost a car. I missed him. He skipped over the stick and I threw my arm out."

Which was important as Damon played a good third base for the Woodlawn cops. He turned to serious golf and won the Chicago amateur city championship in Jackson Park. He became far better known as a golfer than for any achievements during an unremarkable career which began in the south-side and ended there after three shifts ordered by different superintendents.

Financially desperate Chicagoans survived those depression years by clinging together. Two, sometimes three families, crammed themselves into one and two-bedroom flats in ancient build-ings that would have been torn down in better times. Somehow cash was raised for skimpy meals, rent, and utilities. Electricity was used sparingly. There was hunger. School kids paid two cents for a carton of milk. It was free if they couldn't come up with the pennies.

Franklin Roosevelt's National Recovery Act was a welcome awakening although the inertia of the crushing decade lingered. The NRA spawned a Works Progress Administration which saw un-employed businessmen shouldering picks and shovels. Musicians were formed into orchestras for bringing classics to school children. A Civil-ian Conservation Corps, the "CCC," put older teen agers to work on projects proved valuable to later generations. Some sons opted for the Army or Navy but there were no "Uncle Sam Needs You" posters in the thirties.

To Leo his grandfather had an exemplary career. In citing Damon as a perfect cop, Leo said, "He was on nobody's tab. For God's sake, he paid for his own 'coffee and.' "

Damon did accept modest gifts at Christmastime. He brought the bottle of scotch or a sweater home to Nel with some pride.

Describing his relationship with shop keepers, he said, "I was always on call. They were expressing their appreciation."

Pre WW II Chicago was worn out from the depression that had torn hope from armies of good men. Thousands more flooded the city from fore-closed farms in the south and southwest,

The city was no "melting pot" as expressed by poet Carl Sandburg. Family roots were firmly entrenched in neighborhoods identified by their ethnicity. The Careys settled in a south-side clan of Irish while other racial groups came together like lemmings. The more well-to-do Jews roosted in South Shore. The Blacks were locked in a miles-long "belt" between South Park and Halsted, and other enclaves maintained by Poles, Lithuanians, Italians, and Germans were outlined by streets, avenues, and park boundaries, their perimeters zealously guarded.

"Not by guns," Damon said. "Hardly anyone had guns among the general population back then, but a Black man knew he wasn't welcome in our neighborhood, anymore than we would be in his. It was a silly and unreasonable, and I'm ashamed that I lived with it.

"This was all pre drugs, or at least by the standards then. Street crime actually went down after Pearl Harbor, caused I think by all the war work. I was exempt because we had Fran and his sister although I really wanted in. How about that. I miss WW II and your dad gets killed in some stupid chase down Stoney.

"Being a cop was pretty simple during the war. Everyone, even the Blacks, were making money, pouring steel in South Chicago, or building tanks and other war stuff in converted plants scattered around the city. The packing plants were booming, too. A lot of their output was for Spam for our troops and sailors.

"Breaking up family fights and Saturday night brawls in local bars was the most strenuous duty for most cops. We envied the guys, women too, making good money, with lots of overtime, but we hung on to save our pensions."

It wasn't much of a pension, even after forty years service, but Damon didn't need much. He had paid off the mortgage on his $8,000 bungalow on Loomis and had additional income from another rental house nearby. His wife, Nel, had died several years before so Damon was alone, but he was active with a couple of poker clubs, and was as loyal to the White Sox as to his church.

3

Leo was alone, too. He was in his early forties when his wife, Jean, died of cancer and an only son, Roger, was killed in a Jeep accident while on army duty in Germany. He became a virtual twenty-four hour seven-day law enforcer, either active on a case or at his Michigan avenue desk. His rank was Sergeant, homicide bureau, but after his involvement with Tribune reporter, Sid Coffin, in the Alderman Petrovich case, and then in helping solve the murder of a protected witness, he was slated for an upward move. He was Chicago's top investigative cop in homicide because of his long and successful record. His passion for the punishment of evil was relentless and unforgiving.

The nation-wide publicity thrust unwanted praise on a man who had only one objective. "Chicago's a great city," he told a Time Magazine reporter. "I want to help make it safe for every man, woman, and child in it."

The idealism seemed naïve to some of his fellow cops and to old-line pols, but appealed to "windy city" residents who felt his efforts and those of his fellows were instrumental in keeping a huge metropolis under control. Perhaps not politically, but at least on the streets.

Equally supportive of Chicago's police department were the suburbanites who earned their livelihoods in the city, and appreciated the protection for their enterprise.

Leo never second guessed his choice of career. He was convinced law enforcement was as worthwhile and as fulfilling a calling as a man could follow.

About promotion, he told friend Coffin, "I really don't want Bradshaw or Phelan's job, at least not yet. I have nothing to spend the money on, and it would interfere with what I really like to do, the case work."

He got all of that he wanted. Assistant Superintendent Wallace Montgomery cleared the way for Leo's availability in all of the city's twenty odd districts. He said. "You're rep for solving the tough ones goes before you, Leo."

This approval from the top caused little or no animosity from fellow officers who, mostly agreed Leo Carey was a great guy as well as a superior detective.

Leo's immediate boss, Lieutenant Clark Bradshaw didn't like the setup at all, but he knew he had his job because Leo had passed it up when Phelan rose to Captain, so he let it ride. Bradshaw was also a desk-bound officer. Leo Carey had proven so successful that for him to work a crime scene seemed overkill. He considered himself active enough in riding herd on the rest of his unit.

Leo met and dined with his grandfather often, and during one session over Damon's beautifully cooked pot roast Damon said, "We gotta get you married again, son. And you're way outta shape."

Leo grunted his dislike of the subject. He knew he was overweight. Coffin, his Tribune pal, reminded him often enough.

"Yeah, you're right, granddad," and he mentally avowed to begin a strength and aerobic program. And help was nearby from new friends earned in a protected witness case. He had helped Marti Costello, the wife of a protected witness, trip up the United States marshal who murdered her husband. Marti subsequently married Julius Warshawski, the rehab specialist who helped her recover from a serious gunshot wound. Together, the couple established the Julius and Marti Warshawski Training Center. He saw them frequently after the case, but when he didn't take advantage of their offer to help him improve his physical condition, the friendship waned.

Leo blamed a portion of his diminished fitness on the growing nature of crime in a city in which the drug culture was taking a strangle hold. For this involvement there was usually more paper work than active investigation. All too often, what may have appeared a murder by a person or persons unknown was death by overdose. The murder of spouses as a result of inter-marital squabbles was up, too.

"Guns are a major problem now," Damon reminded his grandson. "It was hard to get a gun in my day. They cost a ton. Dillinger and mob guys had to get along with six-shooters and sawed off shotguns . Now, any idiot can get a gun, mostly illegally. When they aren't shooting each over some silly argument or drug matter they leave the damn things where their kids can find them. The kids kill themselves, and their buddies, accidentally. The parents are miserable about it for the rest of their lives, but the damage is done."

Procedures following that and other tragedy involving a death was routine in Chicago's well-polished system. For many of these cases Leo would take a pool car and head for the site of the mayhem, get the scene stabilized for the crime investigation unit and call the district attorney when necessary. He would usually return to his office after making his own check out of the scene. When the death didn't provide an immediate solution, Leo took over the case.

He was again having dinner with his granddad on the evening his cell phone interrupted a fine Damon-prepared meal of spaghetti and meat balls. It was fellow Sergeant Bob Henry.

"Leo, we have a dead one in the Palmer House. It's unusual, you will want to take it."

"What's special about it?"

"The dead man is Clay Burnside."

"Jesus, the Sox left hander?"

"Yeah. I'm here with Patrolman Gene Simmons. Room 429. It looks like he was beaten to death."

"Okay, I'm about twenty minutes from the hotel. I know Simmons. Have you made the calls?"

"Yes, all of them."

Henry knew his job. It irked him that Leo would remind him of routine tasks, but Leo was his friend, too, and he didn't complain. Leo was his senior by ten years, and when Leo asked Bradshaw if he might have an assistant with solid street experience, Bradshaw gave him Henry.

"Not full time, but any time you are active on a homicide."

Leo enjoyed working with the crime specialists he called, "Super snoops," the men and women who had the training, and the equipment, to cover a crime scene as if it was under a microscope. Leo would hope they might come up with something that would be the beginning of a trail, Anything the killer or killers may have left behind.

What a shock this murder would be to the sports world. Burnside, twenty-seven years old, a three-year star the Sox picked up in a major multi-player and cash trade with the San Francisco Giants, was a twenty-game winner last year and already fourteen and three into the final month of the current season.

Damon had ducked into the kitchen as soon as his grandson answered his phone. He knew Leo wasn't to be called unless it was something worth his attention. He was holding a package with an agreeable odor.

"Meat ball sandwich. You'll be hungry later."

"Thanks granddad. Looks like a murder, downtown. I'll keep you in touch."

Damon knew he mustn't delay Leo who was already heading for the door. He appreciated the promise of a call to describe whatever mayhem Leo uncovered. The door was closing as he called, "Take it easy. The poor guy will wait for you."

4

Leo needed no instructions for finding one of Chicago's most famous land marks. Potter Palmer built his first Palmer House in 1871, but it was destroyed in the catastrophic Chicago fire thirteen days after it opened. He replaced it on the site and it was replaced again by the current twenty-five story building called the Palmer House Hilton.

Leo turned over his car to a uniform as he pulled up to the State street entrance. Another officer accompanied him as they strode through the giant lobby. At the bank of elevators he asked the cop, "Who called it in?"

"Al Durkin, the hotel's security dick who was working late. The body was found by a maid who went in the room to do the candy-on-the- pillow bit."

Officer Gene Simmons was stationed at the door of room 429. Carey nodded to the veteran cop as he entered the room. He stared at the king-size bed while pulling on a pair of examiner's gloves. Henry had come to the scene from his office at Eleventh and State, just a mile or so north of the hotel. With Henry was a worried hotel security chief. To Al Durkin something like this in the Palmer House was impossible. He instinctively did the right thing by calling in the police , but he could see the headlines. It was bad news for hotel public relations.

The trio looked down on the victim. To Leo it was the worst murder scene he had ever witnessed. The tall and surprisingly slender Burn-side, wearing only white shorts, lay sprawled on bloody sheets, his legs stretched for the floor. Leo was struck by the sharp contrast of the underwear against the victim's deep tan. The young man's head was turned sharply to his right, his neck was probably broken. The left side of his face was clearly and brutally bruised, jaw bone obviously crushed. Huge bruises covered the left side of the body, ribs surely broken. His left arm was twisted awkwardly.

Leo said, "Looks like lefty Burnside was taken out by a right-hand hitter." He was not trying to be funny.

Henry grunted agreement. "Whoever did this was just plain savage mean. Pathology will find him busted up inside. From the look of his face, the boy was lucky if he was unconscious when the killer went after his body."

Leo bent to peer into the face, "Yeah, his eyes are screwed tight. Looks like they were using knuckles. What do you think?"

"Yeah. I don't think there was a fight here. To me it looks like an assassination."

Leo nodded. "Any signs of anyone else in the room besides Burnside and his killer or killers?"

Henry said, "The bed is rumpled enough to have held more than one person. When we first came in we smelled perfume. It's almost gone now, but we checked the bathroom. The scent is stronger there, but there is no other sign a woman may have been in the room. Don't see any hair or lipstick, but Forensics might find something.

"Could be all kinds of fingerprints. I hope they find something we can check with the data base. We didn't touch his clothes. He, or someone hung up his slacks, shirt, and sport coat. We have his car and house keys. No cell phone, a couple hundred in cash in his wallet. If a hooker was his guest she probably would have taken it."

Durkin roused himself. "We don't let hookers into the Palmer House."

Leo and Henry ignored the claim they regarded as unlikely.

Leo tapped Henry's arm. "Who was that cop who is good on odors? Forget her name but have Simmons get her here right now. Get a statement from the maid. Talk to the reservations people. Was Burnside a regular patron? Interview every guest on the floor. Wake 'em up. I'll call the Sox GM, Matt Holiday. I've met him a couple of times. I'll let him deal with Burnside's family. Wow, this is going to be a helluva blow to the Sox chances."

Durkin said, "Reservations is closed but I'll check the records downstairs. I don't think Burn-side is a regular. No one from the Sox patronizes us so far as I know, but I'll check that, too."

Leo said, "Thanks. And pull his room tab, please. Any phone calls, food or bar orders. You know the drill."

He reached his hand out to shake with each man, then headed for the door. As he left the room he glanced at the large bed's satin coverlet lying neatly folded on a chair near the bed.

A woman's touch? I don't go to that trouble in motels, and Jean didn't either when we vacationed. We just tossed it over a chair.

5

It had been an off day for the south-side White Sox. It was the north-side Cubs turn to entertain a baseball-crazy city. Back at his desk, Leo called White Sox General Manager Matthew Holiday at his home in suburban Hinsdale. Holiday, just home from a poker evening with neighborhood friends. was sipping a beer and watching a west coast game with his wife, Sissy. He did not take the news calmly.

"What?" he screamed. "No, no, no!"

Leo winced. He could never get used to making these calls, especially late at night. He could never forget the call that announced the death of his son.

Holiday had held his job for almost ten years and was locked into his post as tightly as any professional baseball figure can be. He had produced a world's championship the year before and his team had a three-game lead over division rival, the Detroit Tigers, as the season entered the critical month of September. He followed his first exclamations of horror with the usual burst of questions.

"Where? When? How?"

Carey filled him in with the grim facts, ending with, "I will be following the case from my office, and here's my cell. The usual case people are on the scene, I'd appreciate it if you would call Burnside's family. Did Burnside have a wife?"

"No. I have a Rolodex in my office with personal stuff on players. His parents live in Texas, I think. Oh, God, Carey, this is terrible. Terrible for the Sox, for Chicago, for the game of baseball. Who in hell would do such a thing?"

"I hope we can find out. Soon. You can help if you can remember any personal stuff about the young man. Was he popular with the ladies? Anyone special? I'll need a list of his friends among the players, or anyone else."

Leo remembered Burnside's slender build.

"He didn't look all that strong. I have to ask was he clean? I mean of steroids or any of that crap?"

"Oh God, yes. We are rigid on the urine checks. Clay was clean as a whistle. He didn't smoke . He went to high schools, Boy Scout troops, did all he could to warn about the dangers of drugs and body boosters. He was thin for his height, more than six three, weighed only about one eighty five, but he was strong.

"Re women, I can't furnish much. I never saw him with a woman. Wait. Sissy and I ran into him at the Toddy House on Rush. No intro, they just brushed past. The woman was blonde, wore dark glasses. Ballplayers are chased by some kinds of women, and the un-attached guys, and some married, will chase right back. I'm sure Clay wouldn't have gone for the groupies. He was no dummy, had a degree in Social Science from the University of Texas, and I know he was a reader. He always had a book or something on the company plane. He was always friendly, but he didn't kid around much with the other players.

"He might be called a loner, but he signed baseballs and gave autographs. I think all the players liked him, and they knew he was our ticket to another series. He has, had, an apartment on the south-side, near the university, I'll give you the address. I don't think he spent much time in bars. On the road he would look for a public golf course. We permitted the golfers to take their clubs on the plane. Manager Zach Grimes was a player himself and he said if the guys could get themselves out of bed after a night game, play a round and get into the clubhouse two hours before game time it was okay with him."

Leo didn't interrupt. All this might be helpful.

He said, You'll need to call the media, too. Or just the Associated Press. Just give them the basics. I'll have a conference in the morning, I'm going to call Sid Coffin at the Tribune. I owe him from another movie, as they say."

"Yeah, I read Sid's column all the time. He'll be too late for tomorrow, won't he?"

"No, but I'll ask him to hold it unless he is tipped by a Trib press room reporter who may have been there when our Gene Simmons called in. Sid wanders around pretty late and it's only just past midnight. He would have called me if he'd heard anything."

"Leo, thanks for calling me. This is a terrible. I'll get back to you with all the info I can get, including the name of the blonde. A player might know. Or Shorty Cox. He's Zach's bench coach. He's in on all the gossip."

Leo said, "Thanks for what you have now. Call me at any time, twenty-four seven. If I'm not there, I'll be back to you within minutes."

"I've read about you Leo, and I'm sure you will find the son of a bitch who killed one of the finest young men who ever played the game of baseball."

Leo ended the call thinking, "Bullshit baseball is a game, Billions of dollars are involved in player salaries, huge stadiums, and all the other costs. Not to mention the gambling. As much as in any sport, with one hundred and sixty-two games plus post-season action in every American city of any size, Baseball is more a business than most businesses."

He'd try to raise Sid. He and the columnist had been close friends ever since they stood in a near north side alley over the body of City News reporter and Sid's friend Albie O'Bannon. They worked together to find his murderer, powerful Alderman Paul Petrovich. Chicago, the state of Illinois, the entire nation had been stunned

Coffin picked up on the second buzz. He had caller ID.

He said, "Where are you, pal, not at home watching TV like any normal Chicagoan, I suppose."

"No, Sid, I'm serving this vast city, as usual, and as usual you get my news."

Leo gave him the basics. He heard Coffin's gasp. It took something big to move the man. The reporter-columnist had covered the never-ending stream of Chicago mayhem for twenty-five years.

He said, "Oh my God, this awful. I've heard nothing. I could still get front-page bulletin but I suppose you want me to hold it?

"Yeah. Holiday is going the call AP. And I'll call a conference in the morning."

"Ok. Got any leads?"

"We smelled perfume."

"Ah, Cherchez la femme. Hey, Marian keeps bugging me to bring you to the apartment for dinner."

"Thank her, please, and thank you, Sid. Next week maybe? Like Friday?"

"Okay, I'll call. Bye."

Carey returned to his office and used his computer to type out a note for Bradshaw, copy to Phelan. Several late people gathered around his desk. He pointed to the computer monitor as he typed.

"It's all right here, guys."

He saw no point in waiting for the reports from crime scene investigators, It was nearly two so he went home to his apartment. It occurred to him he might live near Burnside. They had his keys and address from his wallet. He would need to take a crew to examine the pitcher's apartment first thing, He was tired, headed for bed, but not before he ate half of Damon's lovely meat ball sandwich with a glass of milk.

6 |

It was an exhausting night for Matt Holiday. Clay Burnside's parents, George and Myra, had just retired and it was a stunning wake up call. George Burnside was his son's high school coach, and his wife was president of a high school varsity mother's group. Holiday could hear the wails of Clay's mother as he repeated every-thing he had received from Leo Carey. The call lasted fifteen minutes.

Burnside ended it by promising, "We'll get on a plane as soon as possible tomorrow."

Holiday promised to arrange hotel accommodations.

"You will be guests of the White Sox organization, Mr. Burnside, and we will help you in any arrangements that are needed."

Holiday found his wife, Sissy, in their bedroom upstairs. She had a cold wash rag over her face and was stretched out on their king-size bed.

Her question was a croak. "Who could do such a thing?"

Holiday said, "It's awful I've had some lousy moments in this job, firing people and sending kids down, but this just makes me sick."

He patted her on a hip. "I have to make more calls."

The next one was to the team's principal owner, Walter Konenberger in Philadelphia. The drug solon had not yet retired. His shock and outrage registered through the phone. The billionaire had formed the syndicate which raised a huge pot for the Sox acquisition. After hearing Holiday's report and voicing his remorse, he said, "There goes the pennant."

Holiday escaped when he said he had to make other calls. Konenberger closed his end by saying he wanted to hear everything the police were doing and that he and Mrs. K would attend Burnside's funeral. Perhaps mollified for the comment about the probable effect on the team, he said, "He was a great kid."

Holiday didn't need Leo Carey's suggestion on the best way to distribute the news as quickly and as broadly as possible. The AP bulletin to Chicago members as well as through-out the nation would be on their wires in a few seconds. A tired voice became instantly alert as Holiday reported the facts. The brief call ended after Holiday answered a few more terse questions.

One more call. Holiday tapped out Zach Grimes's number and this one was almost as wrenching as the call to Burnside's parents.

Grimes said, "I loved that boy. Who in Christ's name would do such a thing? I'd bet my job he wasn't lashed up with gamblers or the drug slime."

Holiday wanted to share the pain with his field boss but he had to get some rest. He ended the call with instructions.

"The team will get the news over TV. Tell anyone who calls I'll tell them everything I can get from the case officer, a Sergeant Leo Carey. You may have heard of him, a famous cop.

"Talk to any players you can get hold of before the meeting. Carey needs a list of Clay's closest friends. Call Shorty Cox. See if he knows of any women Clay was dating. Wake him up. It's important."

Holiday headed for his bedroom after the call. Why did he tell Zach it was important? Jesus! He had never experienced anything as terrible. He was tempted to promote sleep with an ounce or two of bourbon, but didn't think it would help. He'd had enough to drink at poker. He took a long hot shower instead, then climbed into bed to share his despair with an equally horrified wife.

7

Leo got to the office about 7:30, not very refreshed. He booted up his computer. His first task would be to check the night log and learn the extent of work performed after his departure.

Burnside's body had been moved to the morgue. An autopsy was scheduled that morning as soon as the chief pathologist would be available. The man, Dr, Herman Swithold, insisted on hand-ling any dead ones of prominence. Leo thought he was a glory hog.

Forensics would submit a preliminary report that morning. The DA would expect a call as soon as possible after Swithold's report,

Okay. Leo brewed coffee and scarfed the other half of Damon's meat ball sandwich. A message from Henry included news that the maid who discovered the body, Muriel Estaban, ran from the room screaming as soon as she saw Burnside on the bed. She said she saw no one in the hallway, and saw no one enter or leave 429.

Durkin reported that a Melvin Stewart was registered for 429 and that Burnside had never before stayed at the Palmer House. He also reported there were no telephone or room service charges against the room. Nor did Burnside run any charges from any either of the hotel bars.

Another Henry memo-report said he was able to get Charlotte Reno from her near north south-side home to come in for the scent check. Leo remembered the computer specialist from her complaints about cigar smoke in the department's public areas.

"She thought it might be one of two scents, a Parisian Nights or Temps d'April. She said they were popular with young women who might be flirtatious."

Flirtatious, huh. Okay. He picked up his phone. It was Phelan.

"Helluva night, Leo. Why didn't you call me or Bradshaw?"

"And destroy your sleep, too. What for?"

"Well, the Super woke me up. He got saw the shocker from his favorite TV news. Who did you have on the scene"

"Henry. He called it in after patrolman Gene Simmons followed up on the 911."

"Any leads?

"A scent of perfume. A woman might have been in the room according to our best smeller, Charlotte Reno. Charlotte said the lady might be flirtatious.

"Oh, my God. Flirtatious my ass."

Leo laughed. "Well, if it can help her love life we can buy her a bottle."

They hung up after Phelan told his best cop to push the Forensics report.

8

Leo was on the phone steadily for the next hour. The District Attorney call was the briefest. An assistant, Donald Caulfield, also got the news via television, and said he just wanted to be kept in touch. Leo told him he would send him the pathologist's report asap, also anything special from Forensics.

The call from the morgue came in first. It was Swithold who chose to make the call himself.

"Just finished up on your dead pitcher, Sergeant. He was choked to death. Had to be two killers, one holding him from behind, the other doing the vicious hitting. He was as cruelly abused as any victim I've ever examined. I'm sure you noted that in your initial examination, but did you know the killers almost tore his left arm off at the shoulder. Yes, along with broken ribs and a crushed jaw, the brutes chose to mutilate the young man. Had he survived the beating, he would never have pitched again. Oh yes, he had ejaculated, but Forensics didn't find a condom.

"He hadn't been dead for very long when he was found, perhaps a couple of hours. So no rigor. He had eaten a steak dinner, but there was no evidence of alcohol or drugs."

Leo thanked the doctor, then told his administrative assistant, Carole Olson, who had just come in, that he would speak to the media in an hour. She left her desk to take that news to the newspaper, radio, and television reporters gathering in the media room.

Leo would go into the room prepared to describe the situation, but he was always ready to step aside and introduce Phelan or another senior, or even the Superintendent should he be in the room.

He would need to be the department's spokesperson in this case because of the call from Elmer Sharp of Forensics just before he was leaving his desk.

Sharp said, "We have female hair, blonde, a smear of lipstick off a pillow, and semen from Burnside although no condom. Lots of finger-prints in the room, of course. We'll check them out and keep you in touch."

"The hair was blonde? Head hair?"

"Yeah, quite long. Definitely from a female head."

Leo didn't expect to see Sid Coffin in the room. His friend would still be in bed, but a police reporter from the Tribune was in the unusually crowded space down the hall from the squad room.

Captain Phelan was standing at the back of the room alongside Assistant Superintendent Wallace Montgomery, Leo nodded in their direction. They made no move to step forward. It was their tacit approval for Leo to go ahead.

Leo had addressed media groups many times. After his experiences with Coffin he was pretty much at ease with media people. He didn't trust them all. Coffin's warned him.

"It's no more civil than a hundred years ago. We'd cut our best friend's throat for a beat."

Swithold, usually on hand to describe his findings, wasn't in the room. Leo adjusted his notes on the lectern.

"Only one murder of note in this great city last night ladies and gentlemen, but it is a tragic loss to Chicago, to the Chicago White Sox, to baseball and the world of sports, and to Clay Burnside's family.

"I'll tell you what I know, but I won't speculate.

"Chief pathologist, Dr. Swithold, told me this morning that his autopsy revealed Burnside was choked to death and 'cruelly abused,' the doctor's words, and that the injuries inflicted by two persons included a left arm that was literally torn from its socket. His jaw was smashed along with several broken ribs. Swithold said Clay Burnside would never have thrown a ball again, not as a professional pitcher, anyway."

Leo paused at the audible gasps caused by his last revelation. The news the baseball super star would never again be seen in a baseball uniform had special impact now that the agonies he suffered had been verified.

"Smithold said one attacker held Burnside with an arm around neck while killer number two did the hitting."

He looked over a room he had never seen more crowded. "I'm open for questions."

He had always tried to play it straight with the media, but he decided he would have to dance around the lead-off from Ted Kesey of WBFP-TV (World's Best Family Programming). Kesey was the station's chief reporter for their late afternoon roundup

"Sergeant, was anyone with Burnside in room 429 before or after the attack?"

Leo was ready. Had he admitted there was a woman in the room his investigation would be in trouble before it began.

He lied, "May have been, but we can't confirm that at this time."

Kesey jumped in with a follow up before Leo could point to another questioner.

"Well, can you say why he may have been doing a solo act in the Palmer House?"

Leo said, "I haven't the slightest idea."

Others who may have asked the same question saw that Carey was not about to elaborate. The questions veered into less sensitive areas for several more minutes.

He was then led aside by the television reporters who repeated some of the questions for their reports. Phelan and Montgomery stood in camera view behind Leo as he went through this routine.

"Just so the public knows CPD is involved all the way to the top," Phelan explained at a long- ago session.

The group broke up quickly, but Montgomery whispered something to Phelan and the Captain took Leo's arm as they walked back to the squad room.

"The super would like to see us in about five minutes. I thought you handled that very well, but he will want to discuss coverage."

Mangano's office was a couple of floors up. Leo and Phelan were met at his door by Lieutenant Bradshaw. Bradshaw had not attended the press conference. Leo presumed he was on some other task, although Bradshaw generally avoided such functions when Leo officiated.

He told Leo early in their relationship, "It's a lot of crap. The public needs to know is bullshit. We would be a great deal more efficient, make a lot more arrests, and solve more crime, if we told the public zip."

Leo didn't quarrel with the opinion. He told Damon, "He may be partly right, but I'm not saluting that flag."

Damon said, "Hey, don't you ever forget how helpful the public can be, and I'm not talking about snitches."

"Right, granddad."

Bradshaw had been promoted by Phelan, but Phelan told him Leo would have first crack on cases both in and out of their jurisdiction,

He said, "He has earned this status, Clark. He will keep you in the loop, of course."

Leo told Sid Coffin. "I can't blame Bradshaw for any resentment."

Coffin said, "Screw him. He owes you for his job."

Mangano pointed at chairs before his large desk, then looked at Leo.

"I hope you get lucky, and quick, in this awful thing. The shock that's going through this baseball-nutty town right now is worse than caused by any riot, anything at all that I can recall. This case has to be solved. For it to go into the closed case file is unthinkable. Phelan, Bradshaw, give Carey everything and anyone he needs."

Bradshaw, poker faced, nodded. The super was referring to manpower. Bradshaw knew Carey would take whatever he needed without asking, but would probably keep him informed.

Montgomery said, "Between us boys, how in hell did a hood or more get into the hotel without someone spotting them."

Leo said, "I talked with the house cop, Al Durkin. He said he has a good idea and will call soon as it checks out.

"He said Burnside did not check into the room. Someone must have preregistered him under the name, Melvin Stewart. As of now, no one saw him enter the room. Not even the maid. She saw him for the first time dead.

"There was the usual traffic in the lobby early in the evening. The concierge, Jacob Alphonse, noticed a good looking blonde enter the lobby from the bar about seven. He said she walked directly to the bank of elevators and entered a car alone. He said he did not see her again before he went off duty at ten. We talked with two bell men still on duty, but neither of them saw anyone other than normal late night traffic and the crowd leaving the last show in the Empire room. Both men left the lobby on other errands before leaving the hotel at midnight."

Leo said, "There was nothing in the room but Burnside's body, his clothes, keys and wallet. Untouched cash in the wallet. If he had a phone, it was missing."

Montgomery said, "So it's cherchez the blonde. Any leads?"

Leo remembered his talk with Matt Holiday.

"Matt Holiday, the White Sox general manager, said he and his wife saw Burnside with a blonde in a Rush street bar several days ago. They passed in the doorway but there were no introductions."

Phelan, sitting next to Leo, said, "Two blondes. Presumably the same woman. Maybe not."

Leo nodded on this possibility, and sat without comment as the men threw out their ideas. He nodded politely after each offering. They wanted to be helpful and he would check out all new theories.

Mangano. "What's your next move, Carey?"

"Sergeant Henry and patrolman Gene Simmons were to interview every resident on the fourth floor, and we will continue to interview employees. I expect to have a report of their findings after this meeting. They also are working with Durkin on how the killers got in and out."

Mangano waved a hand. "Okay, Sergeant, let's break this up so you can get back to work. Your efforts to this point are appreciated, as usual."

9

Leo Carey didn't have an easy time in the academy. His fellow cadets knew he had lots of Chicago-style clout. A good number of them had relatives in Chicago law enforcement, too, but Leo's father, Fran, was not only a friend of academy director Tim O'Boyle, but they were one-time patrol car partners.

"I stayed home with a touch of flu or I would have been driving that blue and White," O'Boyle told Leo on Leo's first day.

Leo knew that, and he also knew that O'Boyle had his current post because he wanted to get off the street.

Damon told him why.

"O'Boyle was close to your dad, and he told Fran he was considering leaving the force. Before he switched to patrol he had been on homicide several years and was getting into what is now called depression. What we called the dumps. It can be dangerous. We cops are supposed to be strong and can witness all the bad stuff without being affected by it. Tim was afraid that showing his feelings would have been seen as a sign of weakness by fellow cops and his superiors. That can kill a career.

"In my day we didn't see things that happen almost every day now. I mean the mass killings, kids being thrown out of cars, husband and wives shooting each other. We have cop suicides now. Too many. I only remember two in my career. Those were guys who got involved with bootleggers. Now the reasons are likely related to the depression brought on by the job."

O'Boyle greeted Leo warmly, but he let the recruit know there would be no rubber-stamp approval for his candidacy.

"Your instructors will be pushing you hard, Leo. We've had sons of other officers who died on duty. We can't show favoritism. I'm sure you are going to do well, but if you have any trouble, now or later on in your career, give me a call."

Leo expected to work hard. He earned top ratings in every course, showing special aptitudes in small arms and athletic skills. At 6-3, 220, he surprised supervisors and fellow trainees with his quickness. He boxed well and showed exceptional ability in other man-on-man combat. A progress report from O'Boyle included the remark, "He can dish it out, but he takes it well, too."

He was hardly sworn in before beginning deployment throughout the department's five main divisions. For the next several years he spent six months each in Administrative Services, Crime Strategy and Accountability, Investigative services, Patrol, and Strategy. His capture of the college youth who sought to unload the body of a drugged coed earned him special attention.

It may have appeared to some observers that Leo was getting a boost because of family background. Granddad Damon who still had a few contacts at high levels didn't deny he had spoken up for his grandson.

"Yeah, I called a couple of old friends, but from his first assignments in Admin right through Strategy he has done well. He'll go high with or without special clout."

"Clout," a word readily identified with influence in Chicago.

Early in the afternoon, Leo Carey met with Bob Henry for lunch in the central office cafeteria. It was a quiet meal, with both men searching their minds for any sort of a link that might help the investigation.

Henry broke the reverie. "Want more coffee?"

"Naw, thanks. I'm trying to cut down."

Henry said, "You couldn't do much with Kesey's question. He and the other pests will keep after you."

"Yeah, but we can try to keep the women, blonde or whatever, out of the news. Once it's released, the lady or ladies will pull the lids into their holes with them. We need some time. I'll try to make it up to Kesey."

Henry said, "Too bad we couldn't get a break from the fourth floor interviews. Almost every room was occupied on that wing of the building."

Leo said, "We should keep in touch with Durkin and the other hotel people. How did Clay get the freebie to the room? I'll keep after Holiday, too. He should be able to get an ID on the blonde he saw with Burnside on Rush. He said Burnside was anything but a loose canon with the ladies,

"If Holiday can't help we may have to go public about our victim with the woman on Rush. It she was his regular squeeze some-one should come forward with a name."

Henry said, "It doesn't fit with what we know about Burnside to date, but the blonde in 429 could be a hooke r. She didn't stay very long."

Leo nodded. Yeah, it's possible. He was a loner and might have a secret life he's been able to hide, but what about the two hundred in his slacks. Did he pay by credit card? Check that out, will you?"

"Already have. Nothing useful. He used the card for some meals and green fees when the team was on the road. Food and gas at home."

Leo remembered the need to visit Burn-side's apartment where they could get his land phone records.

"Why didn't Burnside meet with the woman at his own place?"

Any answer Henry might have had was interrupted by Carole Olson.

"Al Durkin says he has something that might be useful. You have his number?"

"Yeah, and thanks." He punched it out.

"It's Carey, Al. What's up?"

He listened, then smiled. "Good on you. I'll want to talk to him. He on duty tonight? Thanks a ton. Bye."

Henry said, "Something useful?"

"Durkin says a hotel bartender served Burn-side and a pretty blonde early on the same evening Burnside was killed. He also confirmed that the room was registered to a Melvin Stewart, paid for in cash delivered by an unidentified messenger. Stewart, who we can suppose was Clay Burnside, did not do a formal check in, but went straight to his room, I'll talk to the bartender. Did you do paper on the other fourth floor guests?

"Yes, we're covered. This could be the Rush street blonde. Or another woman. Maybe one of the ladies was setting the poor guy up. Some kind of blackmail scheme, Or Burnside backed out of a gambling deal. We've seen some mean ladies in our time, Leo, but based on what we have on Burnside thus far I can't see him getting involved with that kind of female."

Leo pushed his chair back. "Okay, I'm going to try to see Holiday. I'd also like to talk with Burnside's parents."

"Man, you are welcome to that duty."

"Yeah, I hate it, too, but it might lead to something. You make arrangements for checking out Burnside's apartment, and I'll see ya later."

11

Leo met Matt Holiday in the White Sox general manager's office at Cellular Field, the baseball club's stadium at 35th and Shields. It was a first trip for Leo. He was admitted at a door alongside one of the ticket offices and took an elevator to the top of the building where Holiday's well-furnished but not ornate quarters were combined with a special viewer's box hanging almost over home plate. The carpet was soft, the furniture appeared new, and one cork-lined wall of the thirty-foot square room was festooned with White Sox memorabilia, mostly photographs of current and departed stars, also pictures of Sox officials with political figures. Holiday pointed to a chair in front of his desk, but Leo took a couple of minutes to tour the room and review the photographs, many of which prompted pleasant memories.

He pointed at a score card mounted in plastic. "I was at that game. When Kenorko hit that ball out in the twelfth the place went nuts."

Holiday grinned, "Yeah, that's my score card. For some reason I decided to keep score that night. I did a lot of scoring in my fandom days.

I'm glad I covered that game."

"Yeah." Leo took the indicated chair. He said, "I guess you're already trying to find a new pitcher?"

"Pretty hopeless at this stage of the season, even with the commissioner giving us an exemption to deal for someone. Teams not contending for the playoffs don't have much to offer. No one anywhere near Burny's quality anyway. We'll probably have to platoon several kids from triple A, use anyone who might get hot and keep us in the race. We were pretty sure Burny would start another six games and win at least four of them. We lost a lot."

Leo responded with a nod, and the men sat silent for several seconds.

Holiday said, "Sorry, I wasn't able to get an ident on the blonde. Neither were Zach or Shorty Cox. Both men are in the building now for the special meeting with the players. We could watch the meeting from here if you like. We have a hook up that lets me talk with Zach in his office. Saves him making the hike up here. The camera can cover the entire locker room as well."

"Hey, how about that. Anyone claim invasion of privacy?"

Holiday smiled. "No, but the young men know of the hook up. It might save us some money in torn up towels and other damages after close games."

"They hate to lose, huh?"

"Oh yeah. Zach and his coaches lead the gloom. I like it. We promote saving emotion for the games, but we don't discourage letting off steam after a loss."

Leo said, "I'll take a pass on the meeting, but I would like to meet with Grimes. How about the parents? Are they in the city?"

"They will be in the Hilton on Michigan this evening. I've volunteered to help with funeral arrangements tomorrow. I could set up a meeting for you."

"Yes, please. I'll be available any time."

12

Holiday escorted Leo to the locker room and introduced him to Zach Grimes. Grimes's led Leo into his office and Holiday excused himself.

Grimes, a tall man with a thatch of snow white hair, had pitched successfully in major league baseball for fifteen years before beginning his twenty-year coaching and managing career. He had retained most of the condition of a former professional athlete, but he was clearly not a happy man. He sat hunched over behind his desk, his hands busy fiddling with some objects. He looked up at his visitor and tried to smile.

He said, "That meeting with Matt and the team was the lousiest thirty minutes I've ever spent in baseball."

Leo nodded. He would let Grimes let it all hang out.

Grimes said, "Burny was special. I had a wonderful relationship with the boy because I was a pitcher, too, and appreciated what he had accomplished. He was going to be one of the great ones. He had it all."

Leo said, "Was he popular among the players?"

"Oh they all liked him, but not as pals or drinking buddies. He didn't have a player buddy, and didn't drink so far as I know. And he didn't swap jokes or snap towels. He was their bread and butter. They saw him as taking them to the big money. You know what happens to a major league payroll with a pennant or world series winner."

Leo nodded. It wasn't unthinkable that gambling interests could have wanted to shorten the odds on the Sox. Wrecking his arm might have been meant to sell that idea, but they didn't have to kill the poor guy."

Grimes then saved him from asking his next question.

He said, "He didn't have friends dropping in the locker room or people bugging him for tickets. He just came to the park like anyone else would go to the office. He didn't get to the locker room early, or stay late. He just did his job and went home. At least I think that's where he went."

"Holiday said he kept pretty much to himself on the road, too."

"Yeah, Shorty and I played golf with him and saw some movies together. He read a lot. Ball-players as a rule don't read much more than sports pages. Afraid it hurt their eyes, but when we were on the road, in an airplane, Burny had his head in a book most of the time."

"Ever see him with people you didn't know?"

Grimes didn't like the question.

"You thinking about gamblers? Hell no. And he didn't go for the groupies, either. The man was totally clean."

Leo guessed coach Cox would probably uphold his boss's views. That interview could wait. He stood up. He had all he needed, at least for now.

"You've obviously lost a friend as well as a super player, Zach. I'm sorry and can only hope you can carry on for the best possible season under the circumstances."

Grimes stood, too, perhaps unhappy over his tart response to Leo's question about strangers in Burnside's life.

"I hope you can find the son of a bitch, and soon, Sergeant."

Leo reminded himself that Holiday's office would have made a nice walk from his office on State. He really had to do more to stay in shape. Sox Manager Grimes, the former pitcher, looked very fit for a guy approaching sixty.

Carole Olson had a note from Holiday and left two calls on the spindle.

"Sid Coffin and a guy who said he had something in connection with the Burnside matter. I've bounced several of these to Henry, but this one, from a Minneapolis area code, sounded like it might be worth your personal handling."

Olson, an aide for fifteen years, and saving up for a son's college education, could read more out of a phone message than most people get out of a Sunday newspaper.

Leo said, "Okay, try to get him."

He riffled through the other call memos. Nothing he couldn't get to later. Sid would have a reminder for the dinner date with him and Marian. He would look forward to that. She could really cook. He paused over the memo from Matt Holiday. It said, "George and Myra Burnside are in room 226 at the Hilton. They await your call."

Carole got an answer on the Minneapolis number. He picked up.

"Sergeant Leo Carey here. You have some-thing for me. First, give me a name, please."

"Prefer not to do that right now, Sergeant," said the husky voice, "but I was a fourth floor guest in the Palmer House when

Burnside was killed. I checked out late that night for a meeting the next day in Minneapolis. I saw the news on television."

"Okay, what did you see?"

"I saw a blonde woman in the hallway. I had been picking up some ice in the service alcove and was just stepping back into the hall when I heard a door close. For some reason I took a peek around the corner. The woman was walking away from me, fast. I can't describe her. She seemed of moderate height, slender figure in a brown cloth coat.

"How far down the hall was she?"

"Maybe forty or fifty feet."

"Can you give me any more on her description?"

"All I saw was her back, the short blonde hair, and the brown coat. She walked well."

"Thank you, sir. That is helpful. Now I will need your name and home address. Phone, too, please."

That tip had been provided by a Norman Califerro. He lived in St. Louis which was a break, Leo thought, not that far away. He thanked Califerro and promised not to call him until he absolutely had to.

Henry was not at his desk, but Leo left a message. "A blonde confirmed, but no ID." He then called Phelan with the same news.

Now for Sid. It was late enough in the afternoon for the late night reporter to be awake.

"Leo, where have you been? I left word an hour ago."

"Hey, Sidney, I have more to do than answer your calls."

Coffin hated the use of his full first name, but he ignored his pal's rebuke.

Leo said, "I just thought you'd like to know that Al Durkin tipped me that Burnside met with a blonde at a Palmer House bar early in the evening he was killed. I've also had a call from a guest who saw a blonde in the hallway about the time Burnside was assaulted and killed. No ID. We also have the word of the concierge who saw a blonde enter a elevator the night of the murder. Neither he nor his two bell men saw her leave the building, That's all I can confirm right now. You'll have it in tomorrow's column, I suppose?"

"Yeah, I might go with a brief mention of a blonde in the Burnside case. I'm not surprised you didn't mention all this at your media gathering this morning."

"Didn't have the call from the guest to confirm the blonde was on Burnside's floor until a few minutes ago. As a matter of fact I hope you'll hold up on this. I don't need the rest of Chicago's news fraternity on my back."

"Okay. Are we on for dinner Friday?"

"Looking forward to it. Bye."

Leo glanced at his watch. He'd better try to see the Burnsides.

He punched the intercom for Carole. "Try to get the Burnsides for me?"

Leo didn't shirk the task which he regarded as the most difficult for a police officer. The looks of disbelief, then shock were unforgettable. Leo had met with bereaved parents, and grandparents, and too often with single parents who were almost children themselves.

There was a youngster, Aldemon Martin, very popular with his high school mates, captain of the Woodlawn basketball team, and a top student, who was shot to death while walking home alone after a meeting with his school counselor. The boy must have been overjoyed with the news he was about to deliver to a grandmother who had raised him from babyhood. He had just been told he was to receive a full four-year scholarship to North-western University. The case went unsolved until after Leo spoke to an assembly of students at the murdered boy's school. He was filling in for another officer who was ill.

He wasn't surprised that his audience of several hundred boys and girls was one hundred per cent Black and Latin, His hope was to inspire one or more of those kids to learn who shot Aldemon and call it in.

He began by describing the murdered boy and the news he was taking home to his grandmother .

"Can't you imagine the thrill for the woman who devoted her life to Aldemon's well being after the death of his parents?"

He thought he might try a new appeal to this audience,

He said, "I remember the words from a poem I read in school. I only remember the beginning . Only a few words. I'll bet some of you could recite it all. My poet, I've forgotten his name, wrote, 'No man is an island.'

Leo paused for what he hoped was dramatic effect.

"I hope you accept that as true. We are all involved in what takes place in our community. If someone among you could lead us to the murderer if this fine young man, it would not only solve a case, but it would pass the word to other would-be killers that they aren't going to get away with it, that all of us will protect each other."

A few days later an anonymous call turned in the killer, a teen-age high school dropout. Reason for the attack, the victim had refused to join a neighborhood gang.

Leo told Sid, "As stupid as that."

Carole made the Burnside call. "They will be available and will meet with you about 8 p.m. in their room."

Leo did some paper shuffling and called Henry about the Califerro call.

"It checks out with what we have. I'm going to get something to eat and then see the Burnsides at the Michigan Hilton. I'll try to work in the Rush street bar where the Holidays saw Burnside with a blonde".

Leo had grown used to eating alone. He didn't care to prepare meals for himself other than coffee and cereal breakfasts, fast-food restaurants, and dinners he could microwave. Dining out he usually selected restaurants close to his apartment. The Bear on 55th was one of them. and he remembered the rib eye steak he ate there a couple of weeks ago. It would do for a repeat.

The bar-restaurant was quiet with the bar almost empty and just a few diners. Leo was greeted by the bar's owner and greeter, Sal Baiano, who could never forget and often reminded Leo of his reckless heroism in the Kathy Schultz case of more than twenty years before. Baiano had run into the alley to see Leo's dive onto Jeffrey Blanchard's truck.

Sal had gained weight out of proportion to his short height over those years, a fact Leo would sometimes mention before Sal teased him about his own expanded girth.

"Leo, m'man. How ya doin?"

"I'm doing okay, round man. You gotta steak worth eating in that moldy ice box?"

"You kidding? Rib eye, medium rare, right? Go sit in your booth and it'll be ready in ten minutes. You want a beer, coffee?"

Leo chose coffee although a beer would have tasted good. He didn't want to smell of alcohol at his Burnside meeting, but he hoped they had something. It might help to ease the formality and tension of their interview with a police officer.

Corrine was his waitress. She was in her middle thirties, blonde and pretty, also bright. Among other reasons Leo liked her was her uniform, always brilliantly white, and spotless. He also admired the way she fit in it. He was impressed, too, by her educational interests. She audited courses in psychology at the university.

She and Leo had maintained a cautious friendship over the several years since Leo's widowhood. She was single, divorced. Leo had considered asking her for a date, but he was afraid it might lead to a commitment he didn't want. He wasn't about to get too close to any female. He still longed for Jean, but told himself that getting buried in his work wasn't the answer to living out his days. He needed a self sales job that included ladies but he couldn't quite pull it off. Yet.

Corrine brought the coffee. "Good evening, my favorite cop. What kind of day did you have? Catch any bad people?"

Leo noted her reference to "people." Corrine was nonsexist.

"Not bad, not bad. How about you?"

She stood, a hip pressed against the table. "I heard a great lecture on abnormal psyc this morning. It was about single men. Were you aware that bachelors are often in advance stages of tension that triggers all sorts of bad stuff, like going to ladies of the evening."

"You're kidding?"

"Why do people say that when they hear something unusual? The lecturer wasn't kidding. He's about sixty and a Ph. D. He doesn't go around kidding."

Leo was in full smile now. The lady was smart, and funny. He needed something like that. The psyc professor must have told his class a great deal more than she just revealed. Corrine was no innocent. Was he offering him an opening?

She went on. "That's terrible about Clay Burnside. Do you know he lives, or lived in the area, sits in on courses at the U. I sat near him once. He comes in, came in I should say, sits and takes notes. We see him here, too, once in awhile. He would have one beer, said it helped him sleep after pitching. I've served him. He never talked much, but was polite. He was a generous tipper, too."

Leo remembered he needed to check out the pitcher's apartment. He would do it tomorrow morning.

"Ever see him with anyone?"

"No, but I didn't wait on him every time he came in. He may have brought someone. I'll ask Flo and Katey. He was a good looking kid."

A beautiful multi-millionaire corpse.

He said, smiling, "Isn't my meal ready?"

She flounced off the table's edge. "Excuse me!" But she wasn't angry. It was part of the act.

There was no more conversation with Corrine as she was kept busy with other diners. He regretted that she didn't come back. She was fun to talk with, much as it was with Jean who always wore a happy face. He could be on a case steady for several days, not coming home for meals and coming to bed when she had been there for hours. She still remained calm, much different than the case with many cop wives unable or not willing to endure the loneliness that can be the lot of a policeman's wife.

Leo and Damon discussed that, too. Damon said, "Cops socialize with cops.

Friendships with neighbors don't develop as easily as they do with non-cop families. Schedules are partly to blame, but the kind of common- ground relationships that bring couples together doesn't happen easily with cop families. A cop's news from a day on the beat isn't as easy to swap with an office worker or with other more routine job holders. Some cop wives can handle this better than others, but to most of them her husband is the be-all and end-all. When he's talking shop with buddies at a favorite hangout, she is alone with the television and the kids, and not happy about it."

Leo left his usual tip. Fifteen per cent. He wasn't into the twenty per cent league yet, but he paid on the total bill, including tax.

Baiano had long since given up putting Leo on his tab. Deliberately, in the presence of customers, he would say, "I can't buy him a cup of coffee much less a steak."

Leo remembered he had addressed Baiano as "Sol" at their first meeting, and had been quickly corrected.

"It's Sal, for Salvatore. You know I'm Italian, not Jewish. Right?"

The café owner always dressed well, and he drove a Lexus. Sid wondered about that. He didn't think Baiano made a lot of money from his restaurant and bar. He had to pay union scale for the musical combos he employed several nights a week, and the drink and food prices were reason-able or Leo would not have been able to afford his occasional visits. At least not in the early days of his career.

Baiano stopped by to ask him the usual, "How's the meat?"

"Excellent. As usual. My compliments to Louis. Isn't he more than a short-order cook?"

"Yes, and I pay him better than most short-order cooks. He goes through money faster than he can whip up a four-plate dinner. He's gambles, always needing advances to pay somebody off. No other boss would put up with that."

"Horses?"

"No. Baseball right now, but he'll be into football and basket-ball. He's a great Sox fan. He's in the dumps over Burnside."

"Yeah. I hope he isn't getting over his head. I've seen some serious problems. Broken families, broken kneecaps. I'm glad I don't have that itch. Small-stake poker is my limit. How about you?"

"I'm into poker, too, for more money. I need it to run this place. I lose on food. My bar trade is mostly beer drinkers and I don't serve the late night alkies."

"Really. You're too smart to run a business on cards, Sal."

"You're right about that, Leo. I don't play. I just run the games."

"Whoee. Should I tip off Vice.?"

"I know you're kidding Leo. But would you be surprised that they already know all about me and my games?"

Leo gave his friend his rueful look.

"No, I guess not. What do you think about sports in general? Is it clean?"

"You mean the athletes and their management? Yeah, I think so. Baseball's Pete Rose paid a terrible price. He may never make the Hall of Fame. And as I understand the case, he only bet on his own team."

"Yeah, it's too bad. He gave his life to the game."

Sal moved on and Leo's coffee was delivered by Corrine."

"Taking the rest of the day off?"

This might have been an invitation, but Leo only gazed at the lady, showing nothing but innocence to any implication in her query.

"No, I have a couple of jobs that might keep up late." He wouldn't mention the job he hated, the meeting with the Burnside parents.

15

Leo decided he had time for the visit to Rush street's Toddy House, the near north-side restaurant-bar popular with tourists and business travelers as well locals.

Traffic had eased on the outer drive, making for an easy lope northbound during the non-business hours. Leo always enjoyed the lake view as he stayed at the fifty-mile-per hour limit.

Street parking was almost impossible, but he got lucky. A space opened up a few yards from the front door. Good. He wouldn't have to double park. The meter maids were having enough trouble on Chicago's near north-side.

The Toddy House was near some of the larger hotels and the Playboy Club. A quiet night was rare, but it was still early in the cool September evening. Only a few patrons sat at the bar and several tables were unoccupied.

Leo didn't sit. He wedged himself between an unoccupied pair of stools and held up a hand at the tall, slender male who apparently was working solo.

"Help you, sir?"

Leo flipped open his wallet for the usual introduction. "Yes, you could, if you were working a few nights ago when White Sox pitcher Clay Burnside was here."

"Yeah I was. I'd never seen him here before, but I recognized him from TV interviews. It was about six thirty. I didn't serve him. He took the stool right next to where you're standing, but he waved me off. He was staring at the door, and when a good-looking blonde came in, he took her arm and they left. It's awful what happened to him. I guess you're working the case."

"I am, and we need help in identifying that woman. Had you ever seen her before?"

"No. So far as I know she'd never been here before."

"Any other Toddy employees might help?"

"I don't know. Maybe. One or two of the girls that were on with me that evening are working tonight. Should I ask them?"

"You could, but it would be better if I did the interview."

"Sure, I'll get them. Where do you want to talk?"

"Right here would be fine, but first tell me your name."

"Oh. I'm Bud Renfro."

"Nice to meet you. I'm Sergeant Leo Carey. Bud, do you think you would recognize the blonde if you ever saw her again?"

Renfro thought about it for a moment. "Yeah, I think so."

"Okay, Bud. Round up the girls."

Leo watched as Renfro moved to the service end of the bar and beckoned to two of the waitresses, a blonde and a brunet. One of them, the blonde, smiled and walked down the bar to Leo. The other server had an order to deliver, but nodded her agreement that she would soon be available. .

The interview was over in seconds. The waitresses, Karen and Betty, shook their heads in unison and decisively after listening to Leo's question. Leo thanked them, and they returned to their posts.

Leo had a final question for the bartender., He held his position while Renfro worked up drinks for the waitresses and served two of his customers at the bar. Leo then he raised his hand to invite Renfro back for a final question.

"Bud, did you happen to notice how Burnside reacted to the arrival of the blonde. Did he seem happy to see her?"

"Yes, Sergeant. Big smile. She wore dark glasses, but it was easy to see how pretty she was. I think he greeted her by name, too, but

I didn't hear it. They were out of here before I could work up enough courage to ask for an autograph."

Leo glanced at his watch. It was 7:45. He would be a couple of minutes late for his session with the Burnsides. He thanked Renfro and turned for the door.

16

Myra Burnside, short, White-haired, her face showing all the signs of a mother undergoing the agony of losing a child, was standing alongside her husband, George, when he opened the door to their suite.

She said, "I don't believe I'm up to any questioning Sergeant, but I will support George in anything he says or is required of him."

She turned towards their bedroom. George Burnside pointed to a chair and took his seat on the room's sofa.

"How can I help you, Sergeant, but I hope you can help us."

Leo saw another parent trying to hold himself together. George Burnside was in his fifties, tall as his son. He had all his gray hair, and would have been described as handsome if his face was in repose. His forehead was wrinkled and his face was flushed.

Leo had made similar speeches before, but it was always a grind. Somehow he felt more at ease this time.

"First, sir, let me say you and your family have suffered a terrible loss. From what I have learned about your son he was much more than a great athlete. I come to you now as part of our investigation; that is, to gather all facts that might lead us to his killers."

Burnside said. "The news reports said there was more than one."

"Yes, Clay was held by one of the thugs while he was attacked by another."

Burnside lowered his head, shaking it like a fighter trying to force away the cobwebs

"Clay wasn't much of a fighter. I recall only a couple of scrapes he had as a kid, and they were quickly broken up. He did his fighting with his athletic skills. I coached him in baseball, basket-ball, too. He was also a great quarterback. He had to choose between football and baseball. Frankly, baseball offered him more money."

Leo said, "We hear that he wasn't much of a party guy..."

Burnside interrupted. "Heck, he didn't have time. He worked hard, did well in his schoolwork, too. He did some of the obligatory social things. He had to go to the senior prom because his classmates elected him King for the event. His mother had to teach him how to dance. That was funny. He was quick as a cat on his feet, but how we laughed as he wrestled with some simple dance steps."

The last part of the sentence was accompanied by the beginning of a smile, but remorse took over. His face failed to light up.

Leo said quickly, "We learned he was in social studies in college. Where was this, sir?"

Leo knew about the social studies from Matt Holiday.

"He graduated from Texas at Austin. He was strictly baseball there, but he finished his undergraduate work in three years. He would have gone for a master's but the Giant organization offered him a fine bonus."

Leo was beginning to visualize an athletic nerd, a remarkable young man who was only twenty-seven, but going on forty in maturity.

Burnside said, "Call me George, will you, Sergeant? My heart is broken but I still prefer being at ease in conversation."

Leo fought back a sudden flush of moisture in his eyes. He blinked and said, "Sure, of course. And I'm Leo."

Burnside stuck his hand out, and they looked fully into each other's faces for the first time as they exchanged a firm shake. Leo made a great many decisions about people. He thought, "This man had a hell of a lot to do with the development of his son."

"George, could you think of an outstanding characteristic in your son's character or personal code. I mean, did he give you any clues as to strong feelings about any special thing?"

Burnside leaned back in the sofa. Leo thought his look may have been an assessment by a Texas Methodist for an Irish Catholic cop's ability to understand the answer he was about to give. It took him several seconds to begin an answer to Leo's question.

"Leo, our son had a side to him that didn't always go well with the environment in which he grew up. Somehow he became a champion of the underdog. In Texas, a Black person or a Latin is still inferior to Whites in the eyes of many Texans. If not in an aggressive sense, surely in hidden attitudes. As a teacher and coach, I've found this a challenge to work with. Black and Latin athletes have been the nucleus of many of my best teams, and my White players respected that talent, but with some there was always a reserve off the playing field I couldn't change with dynamite."

Leo nodded his understanding.

"I think I know where you're going George. Please go on." Burnside was clearly relieved.

He said, "As a kid Clay had Black and Mexican pals. I mean they were together all the time. They tested his athletic skills, and I believe he inspired them to do well in school. At least they stayed eligible for sports.

"It wasn't just into athletics. He went to their homes, ate their food, and he brought his pals into our home. We were proud of Clay for this and hoped he would find acceptance of his attitudes wherever he went throughout his lifetime.

"But he was tested. Two incidents shook him badly. In San Francisco he was robbed at gunpoint by a Black man. He didn't report the matter. Told us by phone that he thought it was an exceptional case, that the city's crime rate was well under control and he didn't want to ignite racial tension because of his prominence as a well-known ballplayer. But there was a repeat in Chicago near his apartment last year.

It was another stick-up, a Black kid Clay said was clearly on drugs. Clay tried to calm the boy, but he slashed Clay across the chest and ran. Clay had to be sewn up at the university hospital."

Leo said, "I hadn't heard..."

"That's because Clay convinced the Black police officers attending him that it shouldn't be reported. However, he was able to furnish a

description of the robber who several months later was found dead of an overdose."

Leo thought Clay must have done some kind of persuasion to keep that incident off the books.

Burnside wanted to say more on the matter.

"We wanted him out of his south-side apartment, but Clay insisted it was a freak incident, that both the Chicago police and university security people cover the area, and they insist they have this kind of crime under control. Also, he wanted to audit some of the university courses. I really think he was thinking about a post-baseball career in some kind of social work."

That remark about the future did it. For both men. Leo hated himself for his loss of composure, but Burnside was fumbling for a handkerchief as tears fell from his eyes. Leo stood up, held up a hand to signal he was finished with his questions, and moved for the door.

Dabbing at his face, Burnside followed Leo. He said, "I'm sorry, Leo. I hope I can hold up for the funeral."

"I'll be there, George. We can support each other. You've lost more than any man should bear."

Leo later thought his last remark might have been superfluous, but it was certainly true. Clay Burnside was an exceptional human being. So was his father.

17

Leo was entering his apartment, still digesting all that he had heard and learned from George Burnside. At the door he remembered failing to ask the remarkable father if he knew of any women Clay might be seeing.

Oh well. I'll talk with him again.

He was about to flip on the television when Henry called.

"I talked with both Durkin and Curtis Smith, the PH bartender. Smith said he served the woman a white wine, nothing for Burnside. He could only identify her as blonde and good looking. Wore a brown coat. He said they didn't seem very happy with each other's company, then Burnside slapped a bill on the bar and took off through the door into the lobby. She took a few more sips of her wine and followed him. This was probably the blonde the concierge saw take the elevator."

"Okay. Did he remember anything more about her?"

"No, nothing. She didn't remove her coat so they weren't there to drink. He guessed her height at about five-five.

"Durkin said the concierge sticks with his story. He saw a blonde in a brown cloth coat enter an elevator. He didn't see Burnside. I can understand that. Why would he single out one man in a crowded lobby. He left at ten, as we know. The bellmen who stayed until midnight didn't see her leave the hotel."

Leo said. "It might be useful to know that Burnside seemed pleased to see the Toddy House blonde, but not at all pleased to see the hotel blonde."

"Leo, we could have two blondes."

"You got that right, pal. On that I bid you a good night."

Leo was grateful Henry hadn't asked him about his session with George Burnside.

He might have said, "Bob, I just learned that Clay Burnside was ballplayer outside but a great human being inside, and if you had occasion to arrest him he wouldn't hold it against you because you are Black."

18

Leo had a call from granddad Damon to help wake him up.

"How ya doin' son?"

"Nothing much to report. Looks as if two uglies killed the pitcher, but we may have a couple of women in the mix. Which is kind of interesting because Burnside wasn't a womanizer from our reports to date. Somehow he got himself into something that turned very bad. We're pulling all stops to find either of two blondes he was seen with."

Leo told Damon about his conversation with George Burnside. "I've never felt like that in any other case, Damon. Both Burnside and his son were remarkable people. I have to get closure on this one."

"Well, good luck, and you keep me in the loop."

Leo drank his first cup of coffee in his apartment, then called Henry at his Palos Heights home.

"Bob, are we okay to check out Clay's apartment? I'm going to the office. Call me there."

At his desk a few minutes later he had another coffee with the Danish roll he picked up at Lou's delicatessen on 51st and Lake Park. Carole Olson had two calls for him, the first from George Burnside. She got Burnside on the phone a few seconds later.

"Yes, George. What can I do for you?"

"Myra and I want to visit Clay's apartment. Can you make arrangements?"

"Of course I can. We have your son's keys, but I hope you don't mind if we go in first with a couple of people as part of our investigation. I'll call you within an hour. I hope that's all right?"

"Thank you, Sergeant. We'll wait to hear from you."

So it's back to a more formal title. He might be embarrassed over the emotions he showed last night. Understandable.

The second call was from Al Durkin.

"Leo, I talked with our kitchen people. Two men slipped through the kitchen around seven and went out the same way not much later. Our kitchen at that time is very busy. No one challenged them. How did they get in so easily? Because kitchen people sneak out for smokes and don't relock the door. Disciplinary action is in order, but our management will hesitate to fire an entire staff of kitchen people and waiters."

"Thank you, Al. This is important news. We'll pick up a statement later."

Henry called.

"We can go in, Leo, with Forensics. The DA is sending some-one to keep us from stealing anything."

"Okay. See you there in half an hour."

Good re Forensics, Leo thought. They wouldn't expect to find a crime scene, but they might come up with something useful, maybe some hair in Clay's bed.

Leo finished his Danish with another cup of coffee. He would have Henry stay at the apartment to help to help George and Myra with arrangements for their son's clothes, furniture and apart-ment furnishings.

Clay Burnside's apartment at 52nd and Maryland was in a new building by the standards of the area. Built in the late nineties a garage took up the first three-levels. Leo found a visitor's space on the first level and used Burnside's key for admittance to the building. Clay's two-bedroom, two-bath unit was on the eighth floor. Bob Henry and three others were already there, having been admitted by the building superintendent. They had left the door open for him. Henry intro-duced the assistant district attorney, a tall, thin 30-year old with rimless glasses, already losing hair.

"Leo, meet Donald Caulfield."

They shook hands. Leo then greeted the Forensics specialist, Elmer Sharp, barely five seven. in his sixties, but eternally youthful.

Bess Young, the veteran photographer, gave him a wave. Friendly and matronly, always calm, she had covered most of Leo's cases. He last saw her in Clay Burnside hotel room. She was dressed in her usual work clothes, black slacks and white blouse. Her Leica digital was out of its case. She would aim it as directed by Elmer or Leo, or at anything that might prove useful.

Leo said, "You people know the drill. We're here to find anything that might link Clay Burnside with the outside world, especially with other human beings."

Sharp said, "Gloves for any touching, please. Okay if I start with the bedrooms, Leo?"

"Go to it."

Leo was looking for a desk and found it in a corner of the living room. It was a trim piece of Ethan Allen furniture upon which rested a daily calendar, a small Canon camera, and a neat assortment of envelopes, mostly unopened.

He flipped through the pages of the calendar, finding reminders of pitching starts, team departure times, and a dental appointment.

He put the camera in his coat pocket and decided he would take the calendar back to the office for closer examination. He gave the pages, another skim and found a penciled notation several days old. Alone on the page was the entry, "N, 6:30 Toddy House."

He said, "Hey, I think we have a lead. The woman Clay met at the Toddy House has a first or last name beginning with N." He held up the calendar for Young.

With the group surrounding him he sifted through a small assortment of envelopes. He opened the telephone bill, turned pages past the standard charge for local service, and ran his finger down the list of long distance calls. All to the same number in Waco, Texas.

He said, "A few local calls to check. Nothing long distance except to his parents. Carole can check the locals."

Henry said, "Already done Leo, A confirm on a dentist date, a couple orders for pizza, and some book orders with the library. No females."

"Attaboy."

He leafed through the other envelopes. Nothing personal. There was a dentist's bill and an envelope marked Black Alliance for a Greater America. He tore it open and read a thank you note for Burnside's membership renewal and for a donation of $100,000 . He showed it to the others, holding out the page for Young.

Henry said, "Hey, how about that?"

Caulfield said, "Kind of unusual for a professional athlete."

Leo made no comment. The DA's office would know what he had learned about Clay Burnside soon enough.

Leo pulled open the single desk drawer and found a thick picture album along with the usual assortment of pencils, Scotch tape, and a couple of unused memo pads; also a small pair of scissors.

He leafed through pages filled with Burnside as a Little leaguer, swinging a bat and fielding a grounder. He was photographed through an athletic career, posing with baseball and basketball teammate, throwing a football. There were team shots from high school and college, stand-and- grins with youthful buddies of the kind George Burnside described. The pix were chronological, ending with shots of current Sox teammates, and several pages covering his years with the Giants. There were numerous shots with his parents and several with a look-alike male Leo guessed might be a brother. George hadn't mentioned other family. Leo smiled at that news. The Burnsides hadn't been wiped out.

All the photographs were taped in rows. Each had a neatly scripted caption naming the individuals in the photos and describing the site of the picture and the occasion. There were no shots of girl friends but there was a high school prom shot of Burnside with a pretty classmate.

Leo looked for missing spaces or tear outs. There were none.

"Nothing of anyone really close except his parents, No cheer leaders or best girls."

, Henry said, "Well, we already know the man isn't queer."

"Yeah, there's at least one lady friend. Bob, why don't you talk with the super and building manager. Did Clay have any visitors here? How about getting a couple of uniforms to check out his neighbors, and see if Clay employed a housekeeper or maid."

Henry pulled out his cell phone .

The assistant DA then announced he would stay in the apartment with Henry and meet the Burnsides.

He said, "I'm to wait for them, to express the department's condolences."

"Will you tell them I'm borrowing the album, camera, and calendar.

"I see no problem with that."

They gave tough duty to a young department member.

Leo glanced around the neat and tastefully decorated living room. It added to his impression of Clay Burnside as a well-organized man with an attachment to his past via his picture album, but who was nicely adjusted to living alone.

H*e left his place for the last time as if expecting strangers to invade it and judge him by what they saw.*

The group walked into a bedroom where Sharp was finishing up. The technician was gathering his equipment for a visit to the second bedroom.

He said, "This is Clay Burnside's room to judge from the closet, the suit tree, and the book case of novels and other lit. Clean as a hound's tooth in here, folks. The bed was neatly made when I came in and its only occupant as near as I can tell from the squeaky clean sheets was Clay Burnside. The closet and bathroom are routine bachelor, but it's the home of a spit-and- polish single man. A very pronounced one."

While Sharp worked the second bedroom and bath, Leo and Henry moved into the kitchen. Henry said, "Whistle clean. Sharpie should have no trouble finding prints, if there are any besides Burnside's.

"Yeah," said Leo. "I think we are done here. Sharp and Bess can finish up without us. Bob, you'll follow up with the contacts I mentioned. I have to call the Burnsides."

Henry nodded. His affection for the senior homicide detective was only marred by Carey's reminders of matters which he had already covered or had already been given instructions.

Leo's stomach was rumbling. "All I had was coffee and Danish this morning. Anyone want to join me for some real food?"

Henry said. "I'm with you boss." The invitation signaled Leo would pick up the check.

19

Poet Carl Sandburg described Chicago as the city of "big shoulders," but to most serious observers those shoulders carried heavy burdens. The city had seen the heights of achievement for major industry, business, and finance, It supported higher learning, the arts, and major league sport, but it also suffered spells of indifferent government, major crime, labor strife, and a stubborn and enduring racial problem.

The "Black belt," a bleak strip of ancient homes and slum-owner apartment building occupied several square miles of the city's south-side. It was the site of a sub culture which spawned youth whose hopes for successful assimilation into society was often dashed by an array of hurdles. Learning the cruelty of White prejudice was inevitable, but disinterested parents, often a single parent, worsened the problem.

Charged with helping poor children, mostly Black, prepare for adulthood was an educational system which ordered that students, however unable to do the work at a given level, had to be pushed forward. This was scholastic stagnation   for children captured by the thrill of learning and overwhelming frustration for teachers stalled by this policy.

Generations of educators have been confounded by the problem, and sociologists and whomever reigned politically at the time have argued since the end of the Civil war on how best to deal with several generations of Blacks for whom the American dream was best defined as somehow staying alive.

Damon Carey told his grandson he was ashamed of racial attitudes he and fellow police officers held during his beat years. He said the prejudice was "silly," an interesting opinion in view of the history of Damon's own family. Who knew prejudice more than the Irish who chose America over "potato famine" starvation in their homeland. The thousands who poured into America from jam-packed "coffin" ships found conditions in America hardly an improvement. Damon's grandparents suffered in a New York tenement rat's nest until tuberculosis combined with broken hearts killed them along with their two babies and a huge number of the Irish children born there. Their only son, David, fled to Chicago to live in a shanty he built himself with scraps of stolen lumber. Somehow he survived years of back-breaking labor in building the bridges, sewers, canals, and railways that made Chicago explode into a major city and the continent's vital core, Irish energy and love of life along with a solid front against adversity drove them to become Americans.

"More American than Americans" one newspaper columnist put it.

Damon told Leo, "My granddad, father too, had our troubles, with our shanty towns and help wanted ads that said, 'No Irish Need Apply.'

"We took whatever jobs we could get and educated ourselves. My dad told me to go to school or get out and support myself. Nel and I packed your dad, then you, off to the Carmelites. Those priests didn't stand for any nonsense.

Too many Black parents couldn't or wouldn't sell their kids on the need and value of education. Too many of those kids grew up to make bad choices.

"Sure there was prejudice. I was prejudiced, but I got over it as I grew up and understood the big picture. I'm hoping this generation of Black kids can be helped before we lose millions more to drugs and crime and ruined lives."

Leo thought there was hope for improvement. During his years in law enforcement he saw signs of an increasing number of Blacks going to college and staying for degrees. Their improved earnings were leading some of them to flee the city where, if not welcomed by other suburbanites, they at least found relief from the knee-jerk charges from former neighbors that White America was to blame for all Black America's troubles.

Leo became acquainted with the term, "reverse discrimination," which came into vogue with complaints that anti-discrimination statutes
were working against White Americans who might be more qualified for sought-after positions in government and business.

"I see improvement. We elect Black aldermen, a mayor, and congressional representatives. And who would ever have dreamed that Chicago could produce a Black politician who would shock the hell out of the world by becoming President of the United States."

Damon said, "Yeah, some Blacks are breaking through. Remember, they once called us 'White niggers,' because Irish men, and Irish women, accepted any kind of lowly work.

"We didn't like that at all, but somehow we gained clout in this town. We were organized, probably because of our religion, Everything ran through the church and when an Irishman got a break such as a better job, it became his duty according to our church to help other Irishmen. We got into the police force, the mills, the railroads, you name it. Even big business. Look, we finally got a president. Even though that communist bastard killed him."

Leo credited Damon for leading him into fair mindedness on racial matters, but he thought sports might have helped, too. Half his high school football team was Black. The rest had Irish, Polish, and Italian parents. So what the hell! Go with the flow.

As far as the investigation went thus far it appeared Clay Burnside kept his views on racial matters petty much to himself, but to judge from his hefty contributions to the Black alliance he wanted to improve the situation. Leo felt a surge of pride that he shared Burnside's attitudes but he admitted to himself he had done little or nothing to see his attitude shared with his fellow officers.

Bob Henry made it on his own thus far, but the smart, hard-working cop will get promoted if I have anything to do with it.

20

Leo skimmed Elmer Sharp's neatly typed one-page report which concluded that he found no trace of any other person in Clay Burnside's apartment. He ended the brief summary with the comment, "The young man could wear a newly pressed pair of slacks every day in the week."

Leo flipped the report across his desk to Henry. "Which doesn't help anything more than add to Clay Burnside's reputation as a very well-organized guy."

"A neatnick," said Henry who confirmed Sharp's opinion that Burnside was a lone house-keeper.

"No maid or other help. and both the super and building manager said they had never seen with him anyone but his parents. Simmons is interviewing Burnside's neighbors, but my bet is he'll come up with zip."

Leo said, "Y'know I'm wondering why Clay, who from all we've learned thus far, didn't sleep around, or use his own place to entertain women, would choose the Palmer House for a shack up. And the house bar for a meeting place.

"We know someone got him the room he wasn't registered for. Maybe Clay used that source before. Bob, why don't you have another chat with Durkin. He should be able to come up with more on how Clay slipped unknown and unrecognized into that room."

Henry said, "Okay. I'm on it. What are you going to be doing?"

"I'm going to talk to more White Sox people. Someone has to know something more about the man than his won-loss record."

Leo had turned Burnside's camera over to Carole Olson. She would get four-by-six prints. Something Burnside or anyone else filmed might be useful

She came into his office to report a call from George Burnside.

"They are going to take their son back to Waco for a funeral in their church there.

"He said they realize this might disappoint his fellow players and all the others who want to honor him, but Mrs. Burnside has a weak heart and, may not be able to handle the excitement. He has made arrangement for the body's shipment, and they are taking off this afternoon. Henry helped them with packing his clothes and storage of his furniture. He wanted me to relay his thanks to you for your courtesy and understanding. He'll be available for any further questioning, but it will have to be by long distance."

He said, "Let his teammates say goodbye to Clay each in his own way. We will put Clay to rest among his family and friends."

Leo wasn't surprised. He was sorry George Burnside didn't take him into his confidence, but he may have felt Leo might have tried to talk him out of a decision already locked in.

He still wanted to say goodbye to this good man. "Carole, see if you can get him on the phone."

Seconds later he said, "George, it's Leo Carey. We found Clay's camera and will be able to examine any recent photos he may have made. Can you help us re his use of the camera?"

"I'm afraid not. I never saw him use it. He told his mother he bought it recently in a drug store. Less than a hundred dollars."

Leo said. "We think someone in the shots may possibly be linked to the crime, but I'm glad I caught you. You go ahead, catch your flight. I'll keep you in touch. I think your decision makes good sense."

"Thank you, Leo, and good luck. I know you will do everything you can to find the inhuman brutes who killed our son."

21

One blonde sought by the police was quite available but she was unaware that she could contribute anything to their investigation. She was youthful Chicagoan Naomi Stafford who would have been willing to admit her brief friendship with Clay Burnside had she the slightest idea they might be looking for her.

The image of Clay being mauled left her in shock. She threw herself on her bed shaking, tears soaking the pillow. She avoided any further news coverage. She called in ill and didn't go to the office for three days.

She was sure she was the only blonde in Clay's acquaintance. They has seen each other regularly for about three weeks before his death.

They hadn't exchanged a kiss in the friendship that began when he came into the White Sox general office on some mission she never troubled to learn. She had no intention to start anything with the good looking young man, but they literally ran into each other in the office hallway. He later called. She knew it probably wasn't a good idea to date a ballplayer, and she thought it a good idea to keep the innocent relationship under wraps. She was certain that no one on her staff, or anyone connected with the White Sox, had ever seen them together. Clay made no objection when she suggested they meet away from the office or the ball park.

Their dates were uncomplicated. They ate light meals and chatted about events of the day, the conversations spiced with laughter. One Sunday, after a day game, they saw a movie . That led to a second movie date. He drove a Black BMW sedan and usually picked her up at her apartment.

She had some idea of the difficulty of becoming a major league player, much less a super star. She told him how impressed she was. He laughed about it.

"Awful lot of luck. I've had great players backing me up, making the plays, getting the hits in the clutch."

It might have sounded like false modesty, but coming from him, it was a judgment from on high.

The closest she had come to being identified as Clay's companion was when they ran into Matt and Sissy Holiday at the Toddy House. They almost collided with the couple when she and Clay were leaving. Luckily she was wearing dark glasses. She wouldn't have been recognized by her best friend. The Holidays didn't know her from Adam anyway. Matt didn't recognize her as a member of his staff until she introduced herself at his birthday party.

She didn't invite Clay into her apartment, nor did he invite her into his. She told herself she didn't expect an invitation. What for? He was obviously shy. She liked him, a lot, but she wasn't going to risk spoiling things by making the first move. If there was going to be a move it would have to be his.

She brought her camera on one of their dates and they grinned into the lens for a couple of selfies. She had prints made at Walgreen's, but before she could give him a set she offended him with her venomous reaction to a crack by a Black teen-ager.

They had walked to Clay's car after a post-game snack in a restaurant near Cellular field. He was holding the door for her when she swung her legs into the car. The boy, lounging on the steps of an apartment building, spotted some thigh exposed by her split skirt.

"Oh momma, Would you look at that!"

It was their last meeting. What had been something nearing more than a meal-movie status had crashed.

Thoughtlessly she blurted, "That Black bum. Who let him out of his cage?"

Burnside made no comment, but the remark seemed to bring a blast of cold air into the car. Naomi sensed she had reacted badly, and she should have dropped it there, but she couldn't. She said, "Sorry about that, Clay, but I can't stand that kind of thing. To me that kid's crack exemplifies a lack of respect not only for women in general, but for everything in the White America they hate. I'll bet that kid quit school and is either pushing drugs or is into it himself. We have thousands of them in Chicago, most of them on welfare, and you can multiply their uselessness by all the illegitimate babies they'll generate. And it goes on and on."

She had forced him to make some kind of comment, but all he would say was, "Well, we have a President who is Black and who might be able to inspire some improvement in the problem."

She just couldn't keep her mouth shut.

"Clay, you sound like so many liberals who have tried to alibi for Black Americans. Nothing is working and as far as I'm concerned nothing is going to work. The OSON objectives should be taken seriously."

"OSON."

"You haven't heard? It's a movement founded by Preston Beach, owner of Beachco corporation. It's called Operation to Save Our Nation, and he makes a great argument for creating a new nation in Africa for Black Americans. It may seem idiotic at first look, but it's getting a lot of interest and support."

Clay's patronizing smile angered her. She decided she would make no further comment about the organization to which she was becoming thoroughly committed.

He thinks I'm out of my mind. He could at least make some kind of comment.

The evening ended almost exactly as in previous dates. He escorted her to the building door, smiled and said he enjoyed the evening. All that was missing was the handshake she thought had become a little more intimate each time they parted.

Naomi knew her dislike of Black people was based on fear. She had been in terror of being assaulted by a Black man since she was twelve-years old. It seemed to her that most faces published in connection with felonious crime in Chicago seemed to be Black with rape in her opinion being almost as heinous as murder. It was unreasonable, but when her best friend and Chicago Roosevelt University classmate, Aldean West, was grabbed after a late evening class then raped in a van and dumped unconscious in an alley off Wabash avenue, Naomi had been so frightened she skipped classes for a week.

When the Black rapist was apprehended, picked up outside the Roosevelt library of all places, her horror nearly drove her insane. It was several months of therapy counsel, and drugs that finally brought her around. She still took calm-down pills when inexplicably the shakes would come back.

22

Clay didn't call to ask Naomi if he could drive her to Matt Holiday's fortieth birthday party. She drove herself. Matt and Sissy's house was under siege by an army of friends, relatives, and White Sox people. She made no effort to avoid him, but he was obviously not going to make nice with her. He pointedly avoided including her in photos he shot of nearly every one of the hundred or so guests.

She tried to be a good guest, moving throughout the party rooms, chatting with anyone who appeared approachable. Matt Holiday seemed pleased to meet her when she identified herself as a Canfield employee. She met his wife, Sissy, briefly. The statuesque brunet was trying to greet all of her guests, but she obviously didn't know how Naomi fit into the White Sox organization.

She said, "I hope you are having a nice time," and moved on.

Naomi decided against forcing a meeting with Clay. She was edging her way to the door when she last saw him standing with a group of White Sox players and their wives or girl friends. He was across the room but his back was turned. What a shame it was to ruin her friendship with this fine young man. He thought she was a bigot, and she sure sounded like one with her explosion that night.

The psychologist she met with after the Aldean horror told her the fear that caused her breakdown was brought about by a great deal of misinformation about Black people.

One of them, a Dr. Walter Carpenter, told her, "Violence of the sort suffered by your friend is perpetrated pretty much across racial lines."

He came up with numbers that surprised her, but she couldn't shake the emotions that had an unyielding grip on her since childhood. Obviously she had to recognize that her attitudes were not developed out of intellectual curiosity. They were held by the men and women with whom she shared her daily life. She remembered the college psychology class in which she read how difficult it is to change attitudes. Now these attitudes she revealed so carelessly had alienated Clay Burnside, who obviously did not agree with her.

Could she ever become more objective and moderate in her views. Too late with Clay. There was no point in approaching him now . It was over. So was the party for her. She moved toward the front door, weaving through the noisy throng, finally dodging between a Black shortstop, a Latin outfielder, and an Irish pitching coach.

The split was just as well. She couldn't slide into a crush on an idealistic loony whose beliefs are a hundred and eighty degrees from those she foolishly exposed on their last date.

Now she had to hope he wouldn't expose her as a bigot. The Canfield owned White Sox had as many Black and Latin players as Whites and it could be disastrous to be known as a strident anti-Black.

There had been no serious attachments with men before meeting Clay. She wanted to succeed, get big in something, and it appeared it would have to be business related. Friends had suggested she think about acting ("You're pretty enough"), but she had neither the desire nor the talent. She had bombed in a couple of school plays, the roles only awarded for her looks.

Both her parents had warned to stay out of the romance league if a big job was her goal. They said if she was to be a leader in any career she chose she would have to forego marriage and family. At least until she could prove herself in something more successful than making a living.

"You can't have it both ways," Adele Stafford had insisted. "To move into the top levels of any endeavor you have to give it your full attention and devotion. You can't do this with a husband and kids."

If she had been a pooch, it would have been easy to follow such edicts on avoiding romantic snares, but she was man bait, pretty with good natural light blonde hair, knockout blue eyes, and all other features complementing those basics very nicely along with a far better than average figure. Men chased her. She dated a few, had a brief fling with a young bond peddler who was as determined as she to stay single, so no wedding bells derailed her objectives of a corner office with platoons of men to serve her bidding. After she earned a degree in computer science at Roosevelt, she used her father's influence to get into the University of Chicago's MBA program. The advanced business degree led to a couple of jobs that were "down-right dull," she told her parents.

Her father was acquainted with the president of the Canfield group and she was hired as an assistant to the manager of the Cellular field property. The interview with Karen Booth had taken all of ten minutes. Booth's boss had said, "This girl is bright and good looking. Give her a job."

Six months later she was manager of the office. Booth had quit for something "down East where I was educated and want to spend the rest of my life." Naomi had the job with a nice raise. She left her parents safe harbor and rented a near- north side apartment with a first-rate security system and a twenty-four hour doorman. A cab picked her up in the morning and dropped her off wherever she desired at the end of her work days.

23

She was dating Clay when she met Preston Beach and his OSON. Clay was on the road with his Sox. There was nothing on the tube, She thought she would check out the invitation she found in a weekly newspaper dropped in her apartment building lobby.

A two-sentence large-print question message filled the page

"Concerned about America's future? Are you aware of our nation's number one problem? Then you should attend this meeting."

Naomi thought there may have been three hundred men and women seated in folding chairs in the hotel dining room. They faced a small dais behind which a two by ten-foot paper banner read "Save America With OSON."

Promptly at eight a tall dark-haired woman dressed in Black slacks and a white blouse stepped before a lectern.

She smiled, "I am Pamela Kirsten and it's my pleasure to introduce a man with an idea he is sure will help preserve our nation for future generations of Americans. He is Preston Beach, a native Chicagoan and a graduate of the University Chicago in Sociology, He earned a Master's degree in the same discipline at Northwestern university. His base financial holding , Beachco

Corporation. is listed in the top ten of Fortune's Five Hundred. For the past ten years Mr. Beach has researched the problem he is about to describe along with his plan for a solution. He has named his project OSON for Operation to Save Our Nation. It's my pleasure to introduce Preston Beach."

The tall, well-dressed, late-forties man who stepped to the lectern was leading man handsome, Naomi thought, with his appearance only marred by a slight limp.

She was shocked by his first words. The man's audacious idea to transport huge numbers of Black Americans to Africa to form a new nation was so blunt, so sweeping that she had to gasp. She heard all of the "back to Africa" banalities before, but Beach didn't sound like a soap box zealot. He spoke as if he was addressing a business meetings with the eloquence of a salesman well versed on his subject. In a matter of fact delivery he froze his audience with the charge that America's Black population was "sucking the life out of the nation as a whole and Black people for the most part, were being deprived of a normal American life."

He said, "I do not hate Black people. OSON is in complete opposition to ridiculous posturing of the Klu Klux Klan and other hate groups. We respect the Black race, their many contributions to America's culture. We applaud the spirit and determination of Black Americans who have succeeded in all walks of American life. But in terms of our over-all population pitifully few have been assimilated into what they regard correctly as a White world.

"Liberals have tried to promote diversification, the advancement of Blacks in business, the law, and medicine but isn't working to an appreciable extent. According to Sociologist Pamela Newkirk, who reminds us that people of color now make up nearly 40 percent of our population, the percentage of Black law firm partners rose from 1.7 to 1.8 in the past ten years. She reports that management positions for Black men in U.S companies with 100 employees or more rose from 3 to 3.2 per cent in the past thirty years. That's not progress. That's stagnation.

"She also finds evidence of lack of diversification in advanced teaching, apparel, communication, and other fields.

"The subtle and not so subtle forces against Black America are powerful. Our forefathers saw an America where all men are created equal, but they did not see the major racial misfit created when half our young nation welcomed cheap labor for their cotton crops. The tragedy had begun.

"Black parents wanting to see their children have a better life are frustrated by a system that denies equal access to primary education. Too many Black parents do not encourage their children to learn, and too many misguided Black youngsters sneer at efforts to educate them, join gangs and sometimes murder their peers who attempt to do well in school or otherwise seek success in the White world. They label them honkies or traitors to their color and defeatist culture.

"Adding to the turmoil is the huge number of Black men who father children in or out of wedlock, then desert them. Too many hopeless Black women fall prey to the enticements of promiscuity and drugs. Tragically, we now have several generations of Black failure.

"Liberals who ride the guilt train that lingers with fair-minded Americans, lead efforts at diver-sity and seek solutions to the problem, but the numbers show little progress. Our politicians pander for Black votes by making promises they cannot keep. That is. unless these prom-ises have to do with more benefits that an angry White population reluctantly pays for.

"Our contention is that this huge and growing segment of our population is an anchor to America's progress. Our goal at OSON is to help the Black nation in America by creating a Black nation in Africa."

He cited numbers Naomi had heard before, Welfare costs, jail population, and crime related numbers. She had always regarded these statistics as part of the price of having so many poor people failing to function adequately in a largely hostile environment.

Beach said, "Name any sizeable foreign group, Italians, Ger-mans. Irish, Poles. They came to America impoverished for the most part, but today they are leaders in every aspect of American life. Take the less populous foreign imports, Chinese, Japanese, Koreans, Greeks, and Latins. All have struggled to find their niche in America, and are succeeding. And our Jews, while facing prejudice as unwarranted as that shown African Americans, are among the bulwarks of our economy. Their generous support of Black needs is largely condemned by the very people who receive this help. Dislike of Jews by Blacks is well documented."

Hands went up throughout the room when Beach opened the floor to questions.

A senior male said, "We've heard the 'back to Africa' thing all our lives. It's a joke. Africa has its own problems. Where would our Blacks fit in?"

Preston said, "All the Jews in the world cannot possibly fit into Israel, even if they wanted to, but in the case of a Black migration, OSON has already negotiated for the tracts that would host our new nation. Adjoining African nations will gladly accept the importation of Black immigrants who will bring the promise of prosperity to their people.

"Remember, while OSON denigrates the overall Black role in America, we have Black educators, businessmen, and professional people who would have positive influence on third world nations. We will offer these Black Americans attractive incentives because they will be the core of leadership in business and in all the other element of a successful nation. I am a product of the American system. I will devote my fortune to making the best of our way of life work in the new nation."

Naomi couldn't sit still. She rose from her chair, raised her hand and was recognized. Beach smiled, "Yes, young lady. What do you have for me?"

Naomi's experience in speaking to groups was limited to her acting flops. She had to speak loud and clear. She cleared her throat.

"I don't see many African Americans in this audience. It seems to me you have to take your message directly to them. Don't they, as most White Americans, think of Africa as a forbidding place where hundreds of thousands of its residents are murdered or die of disease every year. What kind of strategy do you have to sell your idea?"

He took his time. For all he knew she might be a reporter trying to bait him into saying something outlandish, if his premise wasn't already off the wall.

"Some Blacks have already campaigned to separate Blacks from Whites in America. The idea of Black Americans returning to Africa is also hardly new, but most Black people think the idea stems from White repugnance.

"I expect to speak to audiences with more and more African Americans, and we are just getting underway in Chicago.

"My hometown is Kansas City where the

OSON idea originated. It has gained surprisingly large acceptance there and we have been able to recruit agents who are already describing the idea in major cities. I will follow up and outline the practicalities of our plan including how we can deal with many other problems than disease and attack from neighbors. The time is ripe. Black Americans are ready for our big idea. OSON wants to make the separation more decisive and practical.

"Our movement is based on a simple supposition. We believe we can convince a huge number of Black Americans, particularly young Black Americans, that OSON offers a better opportunity for happiness n a new African nation. We will appeal to a sense of adventure, but incentives would include cash and special training for good jobs with leadership opportunity."

Naomi sank back in her chair. Gosh, the man was ready for her. Another voice; "How do you think Africans will react to all this?

"We have met with African leaders who feel the influx of American Blacks would enhance their attempts to bring Africa into the twenty first century. We find excitement for the idea in the general African American population."

Beach recognized a young man seated alongside Naomi. "Yes sir. Your question?"

Naomi thought Beach might have thought she and the questioner came to the meeting together.

"Aren't you bucking heavy opposition. We now have a Black president. Isn't this proof Blacks and Whites are seeking unity?"

"No, and here's why. President Obama won by a sizeable electoral and popular vote in 2008, and he held on four years later against a diminished and disorganized block of older conservative voters.

"I believe he expected to transfer his leadership to a woman who agreed with his ideas, but the lady was upset by a populist electorate including many Blacks who thought, wrongly I believe, that Obama was to blame for the slow recovery from the 2007-2008 economic recession.

"Our research and it has been extensive and expensive, includes widespread interviews, polling, and focus groups, that tell us there is no definitive improvement in the status of most Black Americans Barack Obama will be likely to pass into history as a remarkable man who as president was frustrated by a congress over which he had little control.

"He was supported by liberals who hoped he could help make significant inroads towards solving of our the nation's racial problems.

"They are wrong. With almost half of the nation against him and his avowed policies, and a congress hopelessly split, he could only accomplish goals most Americans, White or Black, would approve in any administration. I refer to hopeless attempts to improve our inadequate educational system and new restraints on a financial community that had gone wild."

"Who's backing you?" Another unrecognized voice.

Beach said, "Good question. We can hardly succeed in such an ambitious endeavor without solid financial backing. I have committed my personal fortune to our cause and a sizeable number of wealthy Americans have pledged support. We may be ridiculed, but our goals are sound. Our new nation will also help maintain the world leadership of the United States which is eroding at a frightening pace."

One of the few Black woman in the audience held up her hand. Naomi judged the full-figured woman to be in her fifties. She was guessing at her background when she identified herself.

She said, "I'm a teacher, third grade, and it isn't easy. The children are already showing signs of the uneasiness that bodes ill for the future. I'm worried for the kids I judge educable, but see little hope for the rest.

"My great grandparents were imported from Africa and I wouldn't consider going there even if your group would find me qualified, but now I'd like to hear more on how you propose get this huge job done?"

To Naomi the speaker appeared to welcome the question. He was smiling.

"May I ask your name, please?"

"Elizabeth Wilkins."

"Miss or Mrs.?"

"I'm widowed, but have five children, three sons and two daughters. The sons are all adults, two with college educations and well employed. The girls are newly married to whom I consider good men. I believe all of them would consider your ideas sincerely motivated, but preposterous."

Beach maintained his smile.

"Thank you for all that, Mrs. Wilkins. I congratulate you on that wonderful family. May I ask about the third son. What is he doing?"

"I'm sorry to say he is in jail, but not for drugs. He steals expensive cars."

The attentive audience broke into laughter. Beach laughed, too.

"Mrs. Wilkins, I consider you a treasure, and I am so pleased you are here and have raised a question I would very much like to address. It has to do with our criminal justice system and its unfairness to Black America, I contend that it is unfixable. That Blacks have two strikes against them from their first encounter with the law through their ultimate appearance and sentencing in our courts.

"OSON will have a system to deal with crime. It would be irrational for us to feel we could create a nation without lawlessness. but our citizens aren't going to be labeled criminals before they are born.

"Mrs. Wilkins, you are an educated person. You would certainly be welcomed to join the cadre of African-Americans OSON needs to begin its new nation. Obviously your children and their children would be welcome, too. They would be welcome in OSON should they choose to make such a change in their lives. Four of the five represent the American dream. That's an impressive percentage.

"Again, my congratulations. You have asked the question that must be in the minds of every member of our audience. How can huge numbers of Black persons be transported to a new land, and once there adjust to all challenges and conditions of a new life.

"OSON's plan for the first thousand arrivals will be to include the people who can build the basic necessities for the next thousand. Additional emigres will include men and women already skilled or special training to make ready for the next group until we reach our cadre of twenty-five thousand. This make take several years, but then our new nation will be ready to expand.

"Creating our new nation in this way will be expensive for OSON as I and other supporters will be financing the first stages of development. We will be the only source of capital other than provided by members of our cadre. Agriculture and whatever can be provided from natural resources will contribute support for the new nation. OSON will begin the installation of industry and other basic enterprise to help begin trade with other nations. One of my companies which makes transistors, now in short supply throughout the world, will open a plant in our new nation,

"Remember, our government, meaning you and I, have already spent trillions in welfare, food stamps, student loans, legal services, Medicaid, tax and other credits, and anti-poverty programs, not to mention the huge costs of maintaining prison populations. That cost alone would break many nations. Would you believe forty thousand dollars per inmate per year? We do not propose shifting these people to Africa, but we are sure OSON will spur our government, to make far more intensive efforts to keep Black Americans out of jail, and to return as many as possible to successful places in society.

It is reasonable to expect that the American people will want us to succeed and that they will contribute to an orderly and carefully planned exodus of Black Americans to a promised land."

Mrs. Wilkins interrupted, "Still sounds like communistic dreaming to me"

"No, Mrs. W. It's more like the creation of a major new industry. I represent the capital to get the enterprise underway. I will seek out the brightest and most ambitious to form the cadre that will migrate to the huge property already owned or leased by OSON. Our planners, engineers, and architects have already prepared the basic plan which will greet the first residents, hopefully in just a few years time."

She had more. "I'm into Black history and you too must know about Liberia. It began with American help, but revolution after revolution, and other upsets including poverty, disease, and vast unemployment have strangled progress. And the nation is in huge debt."

Beach was enthused with this exchange.

"I'm glad that you brought up Liberia, Mrs. Wilkins. To be sure, the well-intended idea of an African nation created for and governed by Black Americans is in trouble, but OSON presents a much firmer base for success than Liberia. Just one example of the difference, expressed in two words, 'planned parenthood.'

"In the United States, literally millions of Black children are born in poverty and become immediate wards of the state. OSON will not emulate China and dictate the number of children a family might have, but a typical OSON family will recognize that their happiness and lifestyle will depend on their ability to rear, support, and educate all of their children. Remember, our ability to start from scratch enables us to avoid many of the sociological tragedies America is obliged to live with today.

"For instance, we at OSON are convinced the drug culture which is so destructive in America, need not follow us to Africa. Those Blacks already afflicted would not be invited for the migration. To create a market for drugs there has to be a demand. There will be no demand in a drug-fee culture. If there should be a problem despite our vigilance, it will be dealt with in its infancy and ruthlessly."

"I should say something about guns. We will create the means for a national defense, but ordinary citizens will not have or need guns."

Mrs. Wilkins had another contribution.

"Mr. Beach. You must be aware that we Black Americans have prejudices, too. We refer to "White trash" among the population and I believe there is a huge number of Americans we can lump into this category."

Beach appeared to welcome this sally, too.

"You are right, of course. The big difference is that those labeled "White trash" have a far better chance of maintaining or advancing their status than Black Americans in the same socioeconomic grouping.

"Simply being White is the cachet. The advantage is for the White person, regardless of that person's status, economically or socially.

"Incidentally, but importantly, Mrs. Wilkins, as you know, the canard generally accepted by the ignorant and misinformed that Black people are less intelligent than Whites is not accepted by OSON. We understand that any human labeled 'dumb' might be lumped in that status because of ignorance rather than a low intelligence quotient.

Multitudes of normal Black adults, deprived of education or who were not taught with the same diligence given White counterparts, are wrongly labeled 'dumb.' This is mean and incorrect. OSON will combat that hoax and reintroduce education to our new nation's citizens who have somehow missed out their normal schooling, but who are eager to learn."

Wilkins smiled at this inclusion in Beach's message. She may have wanted to respond, but she apparently decided to withhold further comment. Naomi wondered if the lady might wish to confer further with Beach. This was confirmed when she saw her approached by a tall well-dressed Black man as the meeting came to an end.

The meeting had lasted about an hour. Not seeing any more hands raised, Beach said, "Ladies and gentlemen, OSON has enough financial backing to afford lots of coffee and Danish, so please help yourselves. If you are of a mind to make a contribution to OSON there is a basket on the coffee tables. If you are interested in joining our organization we have provided tablets upon which you can write your names, addresses, phone, and E-mail addresses. Thanks very much for coming. I see a number of familiar faces in tonight's audience and I hope we can see you and any friends you might bring to future meetings we will hold in Chicago."

24

It was Friday and Leo was looking forward to his dinner date with Sid and Marian Coffin at their north side apartment. He always enjoyed seeing them together and Marian was a wonderful cook. The day began, however, with a meeting called by Clark Bradshaw.

"Detectives, staff, I have a directive from the top, I mean from Superintendent Mangano. It has to do with the physical condition of our police department. Beginning today, each of you will be weighed. If you are found overweight for your height you will be obliged to undergo physical training in our brand new gym. There are no exceptions. Further instructions will be found on the bulletin board together with a copy of the super's remarks about the situation.

He glanced at Leo who was standing at the rear of the meeting room.

"We must take this seriously. Superintendent Mangano visited our new gym and work out rooms on his own. He told assistant Montgomery that he saw only one person, a rookie patrol-man, working on the parallel bars. He insists we will do a better job if we are all physically fit. Frankly, I agree with him and I'll back him up."

Leo grimaced. *Of course you will, you kiss ass.*

At six-three, 250, Leo knew he was out of shape, but he didn't think he needed to thin out much. He would follow orders, but it would cost him some of Damon's good meals. At The Bear, too. He might need to cut back on seconds with Marian and Sid. He hadn't seen another pair of friends, Marti and Julie Warshawski for weeks. Might be a good idea to visit their popular fitness center, get their ideas although he knew they would talk about discipline in eating habits, and a regimen of exercise, maybe some jogging. God, he hated the jogging. It wasn't as bad as the wind sprints of high school football, but it was so boring.

Naomi didn't feel like coffee so she worked her way to the door. She didn't think she was noticed although she may have been among the younger persons in the room. Just as she reached the exit she felt a pluck at her sleeve. Looming over her was the tall Black man who had been talking with Mrs. Wilkins.

"Excuse me, please, but you seemed particularly interested in Mr. Beach's talk. Would you be interested in meeting him?"

She was startled by the intrusion, her discomfort intensified by the close presence of a Black man. She might have felt panic if they weren't surrounded by the lingering crowd. What is this, she thought, then curiosity took over.

"Where might that be?"

He pointed to a bank of elevators.

"Mr. Beach has a suite in the hotel. He will be along after talking with some of the other people."

What was a reasonable invitation to him set off an alarm to the invitee. No way was she going anywhere with this Black man.

She was speechless, but struggled for control. She might have looked faint. He reached for her elbow. "Are you all right?"

She forced a smile. She could not be rude however bizarre the situation.

She said, "It's been a long day for me and I'm tired. I don't need a long meeting. Couldn't we meet here or in the lobby?"

He smiled. "Of course, but let me excuse myself to tell him you are waiting?"

What the hell. This could be interesting. Maybe she could learn whether Beach is some special kind of nut or really has something going. She was glad she wore a decent dress to the office that day, then asked herself why did it matter. She wasn't dating the man.

She found a chair. Both men joined her in about ten minutes, Beach with his hand out and a big smile.

"May I ask your name, please?"

She told him.

He said, "And this is my aide, Jeremiah Constable. Jerry, isn't the coffee shop still open? We can talk there"

Constable disappeared, and Beach led her after him.

He said, "I 'm about coffeed out, but at least we can be seated for our visit Miss, or is it Mrs.?"

" I'm single, Mr. Beach."

"I also enjoy that status, although divorced. And won't you please call me Preston. I'm even Press to old buddies. Tell me Miss Stafford, are you employed?"

"Yes, I manage the Chicago office for the Canfield group. We own the Chicago White Sox. I make my office at Cellular field, home of the Sox."

Constable met them at the door of the restaurant and led them to a booth. She slid in. Beach sat opposite her.

Constable said, "I'll find Kirsten."

Naomi decided she wouldn't invite him to address her by her first name. The man was even better looking up close. Maybe forty-five to fifty. Expensive cut for his dark hair, tinged with White over the ears. Tall, more than six feet, athletic build, blue eyes in a full and carefree face, unlined but tanned.

"That's an important job. I remember you from our audience tonight, and also your question. Did the other questions and my answers along with my basic talk cover everything you need to know about OSON and its goals."

Constable was back with Kirsten. She slid into the booth next to Naomi and Beach introduced her. Constable sat with Beach.

Naomi asked her first question.

"I'm more interested in strategy now The how of getting it done. You say you will offer incentives, I suppose cash and special jobs for key people, but I can't see how an average Black American, however poor his prospects, can buy into such a radical change. My God, there's everything from terrible disease to mass murder facing them over there. How can your cadre and the thousands that follow repel what will surely be attacks from radical Muslim or other forces."

He said, "You are right, Ms Stafford. Our teams of recruiters are answering these questions and calming fears.

"Regarding health protection for instance. Each immigrant will receive all immunization needed. Our cadre will include the start of an army of health professionals along with a basic laboratory that will be equal to that in Atlanta or any facility in the world. As for the occasional plagues that threaten our world population we will have an enforced shut-down program that will minimize danger.

"About our protection from other African nations or strong men, or religious sects a reliable segment of our cadre will be the best-trained and best-armed in the world. Eventually, every citizen will play a role in our defense. Fortunately, the sites for our new nation are geographically remote from the African nations currently having the most difficulty. Finally, we will have the protection of the finest army in the world, that of the United States. As I'm sure you will agree, our nation's leaders and most Americans will want OSON to succeed."

He turned to Constable. "I'm going to ask Jeremiah to take over at this point. You should have some input from an African-American who is literally the founder of the program."

He nodded at his aide. Constable didn't accept the assignment with a smile. He looked at Naomi as a tutor might be about to establish something he wanted remembered for a lifetime. He leaned forward and stared into her face.

"I don't think you care much for Black people, Miss Stafford. Am I correct?"

It occurred to her she might tell him he could have said that to most White women in the city of Chicago.

She stared back. She would not pussyfoot. "A close friend was beaten and raped by a

Black man, Mr. Constable. I've been in therapy for several months as a result. Is that an answer?"

He decided not to press her on the matter.

He said, "You've had a terrible experience and "I'm sorry." He sucked in a breath.

"I've spent twenty years as a teacher in several African nations. I am a descendant of slaves. I was reared in Charleston, South Caroleina, but grew up in Detroit where my father was an automobile worker. My mother also worked as a domestic to help pay for my college education at the University of Michigan. I hold a Master's degree in Sociology from Michigan.

"I think most Americans view the Black tragedy as beginning with the importation of Blacks as slaves. All too many Americans view the second tragedy as the freeing of Blacks from that status.

"I've held the idea of transporting Black Americans to Africa for many years. Creating a new nation, but getting it right this time. It only became practical when Mr. Beach took over. He and a team of planners have refined the basic concepts into a workable plan.

"He mentioned our research into the attitudes among Black people to help us determine whether a very formidable inertia could be over-come; that is, can a huge number of Black people, however miserable their circumstances and prospects, be moved to make such a difficult and probably traumatic change.

I have talked to literally hundreds of Black people, mostly adults, mostly Americans. Yes, there are Blacks in other nations interested in OSON. I've talked with teen agers, who are ready to go right now. The people I've talked with are in various straits, some on welfare, some barely getting by, some doing quite well, but most of whom would make the move. I've met with lawyers who feel they are getting nowhere as token Blacks in their firms, but who see things even worse should they go on their own. The doctors I've talked with feel they have been accepted as professionals, even as leaders in the profession, but are not all that happy in a social sense. The response from these men and women is significant and positive.

"Parents of young children have been particularly receptive to OSON ideas. They see a much better future for their kids, and for themselves, in the environment we propose."

She butted in, "How about the youth we hear so much about. Undereducated, jobless, crammed with energy, but if they can't hold jobs in labor, or succeed in sports and entertainment, or in the arts, huge numbers of them are lost to drugs and crime."

Beach was ready for this one. "Naomi, our jails are crammed with many of these people. A recent and scary statistic reveals that upon serving their term or being otherwise released, only about thirty percent find lasting jobs. Another thirty percent return to prison within three years. The rest comprise an army of socially adrift and homeless.

"America is afraid of these people We don't know what to do with them. Social programs and job creating efforts only help a few, but we will find the potential leaders, the ambitious, the most impatient, those afraid they are doomed to a future of futility and despair. We can give them responsibility and opportunity. American industry will help us. We are prepared to create new enterprise. OSON will serve Africans who need washing machines and fully equipped kitchens, but also be active in trade with the rest of the world.

"Remember, we will begin with complete control over our economy. China can force its workers to accept the low wages that enable them to dump products throughout the world. They frustrate us further by tinkering with their currency. We will be able to compete with both of those problems. We can harness the Black energy you mentioned to all kinds of positive enterprise.

For our valued teachers, we will build schools that will serve both the intellect and the people who need training for worthwhile labor. Black people aren't lazy. No one will work harder if it means they will be rewarded for the efforts. We will reawaken ambition. As it is now, huge numbers of Black Americans are locked into minimum wage, or less. Both husbands and wives need jobs to make enough to support a small family. Children are often left on their own. OSON may have a ten-hour work day at its beginning, but our ultimate goal will be a six-hour work day, four-day work week. Our goal will be for OSON citizens to have time for fun and ample rest. At the same time hard work and the desire to lead and succeed will be rewarded. Our citizens will own homes, the basis for creating wealth."

She couldn't help but smile. "Wow, I'm ready to go."

He smiled back. She could see he was breathless.

She said, "Will your neighboring nations fit in with your scheme?"

"Yes, enthusiastically. In exchange for renewable one-hundred year leases and outright land purchase we promise trade agreements and the immigration that was vital in America's growth. Many will be needed to replace the initial agricultural and other labor from our initial cadre.

"Basics for our economy will be agriculture and the ability to generate electrical power. We will use solar and wind and new ideas for power generation. These have been inhibited in the states because of the influence of coal, oil, and gas."

She said, "Let me play more of the devil's advocate."

"Go ahead, please."

"I can understand Mrs. Wilkin's thinking you might be creating a communist state. What kind of government will you have?"

Beach's hands made a loud clap as he clasped his hands together. He moved his head across the table as if was going to let Naomi onto something only for her.

"I couldn't begin an argument with that bright lady. It would have distracted our audience from everything said before. The fact is,

Naomi, our start-up government cannot be categorized. As I told Mrs. Wilkins, we will begin much like a new business and evolve into what works for all. A chief executive will function as head of state. The first will be Jeremiah Constable. His African experience together with his years of interaction with Beachco labor make him an ideal choice. He and a small staff will run the show during the cadre years, but every citizen's voice will still be heard. As Chief Executive Officer Jeremiah will issue directives with the goal of satisfying the needs of as many cadre members as possible, much as our president does now with his executive orders. Incidentally, our deposed and current presidents, have set records for executive orders."

He smiled. "Makes one wonder if our congress still has some-thing to do.

"This system may continue as the influx of new citizens begins. As our population grows a cabinet, such as we have in the United States, will be added to oversee various segments of government.

"I will be participating in the growth and development of the new nation for many years. It will be in funding primarily, but as I told Mrs Wilkins and our audience, I will create a new plant for transistors over there. We cannot be a Cuba which has to rely on sugar as its only significant export.

"I hope we can become a democracy, but it will not be a democracy that sees thousands of its citizens slaughtered annually by guns and drivers under the influence of alcohol and opiates."

He paused, raising his eyebrows as to ask if she needed more.

Naomi felt overwhelmed. Suddenly every-thing these men said seemed workable. She could understand Beach's leadership in business. His pragmatism combined with his idealism suddenly made sense.

She said, "I'm impressed with your zeal,

Enough to consider asking for a role in your organization, but I still have reservations. Black Americans, however desperate they might be about their futures and the futures of their children, aren't going to pick up bag and baggage for Africa. What promise can you offer that their lives will be better? Cash and a job offering opportunity will be attractive, but it surely that isn't enough."

Constable held up a hand.

"It will be enough for our cadre, but equally important is the promise our citizens won't be exploited. Manning a shovel for road or landing strip construction is a different proposition when it is accompanied by a wage that can support a family and pay for a house. Also, our cadre laborers can stay with that level of labor if they choose, but they will have the option to train for other work.

"In America we are seeing a basic hope slip away. It's the promise that an American doesn't mind the other guy making it big so long as he can have a shot at that status. Very few Black Americans think that way now. More importantly, they have little hope that their children will have the opportunity to succeed.

"A White candidate for president pointed out that one per cent of Americans have ninety-nine per cent of the wealth and he hopes to level out the playing field. It's unlikely he will see that dream fulfilled. He's bucking a system that has a basic goal of creating wealth, making money, and the wealthy are rarely averse to making themselves more wealthy.

"You don't need an explanation of how capitalistic America works. No one in the world fits the definition better than Preston Beach. With OSON it can work in Africa, but with guidance and new rules because we are able to start from scratch. We are offering the opportunity to begin a new nation to a people for whom America isn't working. Black Americans who are doing well are a tragic minority. Among the trials and fears of the great majority of American Blacks is the fear of an immigration of workers who will work cheaper and take their jobs.

"Politicians who promise to raise the taxes or otherwise dent the holdings of the fortune makers are denounced as socialists or even called communists, and the money holders will resort to all kinds of ploys to safeguard their capital.

"It's only when the super rich decide to share their wealth do we see altruism. That's where the Preston Beaches come into the picture.

He smiled, "Press, permit me to drop your name, as a potential altruist, maybe for funding a new plan to reforest Brazil."

Beach waved a hand. "Help yourself, but let me insert that OSON will not curtail the ambitious, the entrepreneurial, but will be socialist in the sense that no resident will be without health care or the means for caring for his or her family. We will have no 'homeless" in our new African state. Whatever caused this tragedy to become a major problem in the wealthiest nation in the world will not happen in Africa because every child will have two identities, one as a member of a family unit, the second identity as a ward of the state. No one will be lost in the limbo of alcoholism, drug dependence, mental disorder, family discord, or problems with the law. This has nothing to do with communism. It has to do with perfecting the mechanics of how human beings can live together successfully."

Naomi wondered at the effort to impress her. It was more than impressive. They reminded her of the salesman for a Florida planned community who somehow maneuvered an audience with her parents. She remembered they bought a home site and later sold it at a profit. This team was making her feel she might somehow fit into their plans.

Beach had more.

"I can add that we can expect investment in our new nation. Trillions of excess money languishes in money markets or in strong boxes owned by the wealthiest Americans. I call it excess money because only a portion of it is needed for the American economy to function successfully.

Wealthy Americans, and I number myself among them, stay wealthy because we do not allow our wealth to be compromised. In the vernacular, if the American economy goes in the tank, the

Americans with the excess cash may be stung, but in no way will they lose their capital.

"You'll recall the bank panic of 2007-2008.

Ultimately, an emergency stabilization law was enacted, the largest government bailout in our history. Our wealthy Americans didn't come up with the money to stave off disaster. You, the American taxpayer will pick up that huge tab.

"I will be able to finance the basic creation of the new nation, and I have already convinced several of the wealthiest Americans to join OSON.

"We can promise no limits to achievement.

Energy and creativity will be rewarded. An OSON citizen will realize he isn't competing against a White person, who in America is someone better educated or with more influence, such as a parent or brother-in-law, or former schoolmate. That handicap in his view has been removed.

"The intellectuals and liberals and those who already accept Black Americas as equals are outnumbered by those who will never accept a Black person as an equal. OSON offers a practical solution. It can work. If you join us you will not only help achieve one of history's most ambitious undertakings, but will be identified forever as a friend to all mankind.

"We are screening all applicants carefully. We will not take malcontents, inveterate criminals, or the dregs of our society. The United States will be left with a huge number of socially unfit. They will have to accept the problem and deal with it objectively or face social upheaval."

There. He said it. They wanted her, but she had another challenge.

She said, "Our current government is faced with a stubborn immigration problem. South Americans, Mexicans, Asians, even Muslims, want in in unprecedented numbers. These people compete with our Black population for jobs, any kind of jobs, jobs that immigrant Irish, Polish, and Italians took when they first arrived."

Beach was ready. He said, "Yes, and what has occurred in the past will most likely be repeated. Blacks at the lowest socio-economic levels will stay there, or worse. They will be passed over by the immigrants."

Naomi, confused but somehow elated, thought it a good time to excuse herself. She had one more question.

"Are you three all there is to OSON?"

Beach said, "Another good question. The answer is no. We have a fifty person brain trust along with two hundred planners in Africa to prepare for our first cadre. We also have what might be called recruiters in every major city. We have the people we need and will get more, hence my question. Naomi, you are an exceptionally bright and obviously educated person. You've heard the OSON story, and much of our plans, and were a superb devil's advocate. Is it possible we will meet again?"

"I think so, Mr. Beach. You've given me a lot to think about."

26

Naomi hadn't been as excited since fourth grade when a boy she admired invited her to a movie. A man representing huge wealth and power had told her she could help him with a goal that at first look seemed insane, but now seemed entirely possible..

A couple of hours ago, the idea of helping Black people with anything more than a contribution to the Community Fund seemed ridiculous, even laughable. Now she was ready to trade another dead-end job for a role in helping Blacks big time.

Preston Beach didn't promise any special role, but he said her Canfield job was important. Those men wouldn't spend all that effort trying to land someone for a secretarial pool.

She had to discuss it with the only person she had ever given total trust. Her mother, Adele.

She rushed to see her the next day, leaving the office an hour early.

"Mom, Preston Beach is a major figure in the corporate world. I found his story in Wikipedia. He has a bunch of companies under the Beachco umbrella. He has to be worth a ton of money from his family, and he is an only child. His corporation owns banks, newspapers, a publishing business, radio and TV stations, much more.

"It's a huge plan. He thinks America is in trouble the way things are. He wants Black people to succeed, just not here where they don't have a real chance. It was pure luck I went to his meeting, but for him and a top associate to spend another hour with me and offer me a job is fantastic."

Adele Stafford stared at her daughter. The bright, beautiful girl had become a woman of intellect and drive, but where was she going with this?

"Kiddo, this guy sounds dangerous. He's going to get himself killed, and I don't want to see you in the line of fire."

"Mother, I'm not giving up my job with

Canfield, but I might be useful to a really meaningful movement."

Her mother shook her head, "I don't think it's a movement. Yet."

Naomi met with Beach and Constable for lunch at the University of Chicago's International House. They chose the special lunch, filet of sole. Beach also ordered a bottle of wine. She opened the conversation as the men watched the steward do the pouring.

"Gentlemen, I'd like to join the movement.

I'm not sure how you would use me, but I believe in your daring idea."

Beach reached across the table for her hand.

"We are both pleased and honored to know this, Naomi. We took the liberty of checking out your educational achievements, and they are formidable. We can use your brain. How do you feel about creating and placing ads for our meetings? You would coordinate with Pam Kirsten who will be with Jeremiah and me setting up meeting places

"Fine. No problem. I hope you won't ask me to give up my current job, however."

"No need for that right now, but can you

combine your work with a considerable commitment to our cause?"

"Yes, I presume there will be a lot of telephoning. I can do this by cell phone, and I will also use my laptop. My Canfield job isn't all that demanding. My big boss, Walter Konenberg is an absentee boss both physically and mentally. I have no idea how he would feel about my joining OSON.”

Beach smiled, “Would you believe Mr. Konenberg is already a supporter, ready to make a major commitment financially.”

“Wow!”

Both men laughed. Beach said, “Yeah, wow.”

The food arrived. “Let’s enjoy our lunch.”

27

Clay Burnside thought he was falling in love, but when Naomi Stafford told him she had fallen for the Preston Beach crap, he knew it couldn't work.

He was surprised and disappointed with her flare up when the Black youth remarked on her brief display of leg. What the hell. It wasn't as if the kid had said something really rude.

But then she launched into the OSON thing. Of course he had heard of Beach and his impos-sible scheme. My God, he would fight it, even if he had to give up his career. He had attended one of the Chicago meetings. He wasn't recognized. He doubted if there were many baseball fans in the room. He couldn't believe what he heard. This guy thought he could convince the cream of the Afro-American population to pick up and clear out for the dark continent.

He almost stood up and called the guy an idiot. Sure he was a billionaire, and he probably had convinced some people, Black and White, that his great fortune could ground such a movement, but he was wrong, wrong, wrong!

America is working for its Black population. We had a brilliant Black as President. Two terms, and he had impact. He lifted the hopes of millions of Black Americans, along with the spirit of fair play held by millions of White Americans who had been silent supporters of the Black dream. They gave their vote to the man with hope.

After a night game he hadn't worked he called his friend, Allen Cookson, president of the Chicago chapter of the Black Alliance for a

Greater America. He told Allen of his outrage, and what he had heard at the Beach meetings.

Allen had attended OSON meetings. They met for lunch to discuss a BAGA response to Beach and his OSON claims.

Allen said, "The man is not a nut, but he is a zealot. And he is rich. He can amass more money than can be imagined for his scheme. Think of the American business owners who see his idea as opening the gates to unlimited immigration and subverting even more Black labor. We have to come up with counter argument, and soon. I've talked with H.J., who thinks we can hurt OSON with a updated report on the Black situation in America today. Beach's research is flawed, deliberately doctored, of course. America is working for us, and we can prove it. We have the numbers."

"H.J" was Howard J. Showalter, the Ph. D. out of Stanford, who had led the Alliance successfully for ten years.

Clay said, "How's our cash position? I want to release some real money, and I can round up a lot more from athletes, Black and White. who don't know what to do with all their cash."

Allen said, "You've given so much already. It would take a huge amount for a nation-wide campaign.

"I have and can get the money. How do we start?"

A member of our board is one of the most prominent public relations people in America. He could make your position heard round the world. After, all, you are among the most prominent athletes in America."

"Great, when can I meet the man?"

The public relations executive was Homer Carrington who listened without interruption as Clay spilled his distaste for Preston Beach and his OSON.

"The man wants to lure thousands of our successful and middle-class citizens for his so-called 'cadre.' He will be amazed at how quickly those jobs and professional posts will be filled by ambitious and well-trained Black Americans. That's what America is all about. We can fill every open spot with a wannabe in no time at all. Our schools are filled with Black men and women anxious to take leading roles in the American economy. Beach will actually give them opportunity to move into the open slots.

"I'm not in the same financial league with Mr. Beach, but I have some money and I know where to find more to fight that guy. I'm going to start writing ads right now, full pages for maxi-mum impact. I want to use television and radio, too."

Carrington promised to get back to him with a proposal. Instead, Clay learned he had told his plans to the enemy. Carrington was already working for Beach.

Clay told Allen, "It's a kick in the butt. I spilled my guts, but there are other agencies who will be glad to take my money. I'm putting my arguments on paper right now."

"Good for you, Clay. We need your passion. I'll come up with some good agency contacts in a few hours."

Clay had other matters to think about. He had fallen for Naomi and was about to tell her so when she stunned him with her OSON opinions.

Now he had to escape from a far more dangerous entanglement that had troubled him for weeks. It was his affair with Sissy Holiday, the wife of the Sox GM.

Good Lord! She was ten years older than he, but his knees turned to jelly when she introduced herself at a benefit for homeless kids. He always was good for a contribution at these things, but at this one he fell for the big boss's wife.

There were other meetings at one function or another, and the parties after the Series win. She was always there, long Black hair, the looks, posture , and movements of a model. He couldn't take his eyes off her. The glances between them became looks and the looks became longer.

The direct contact began when they were standing aside from a group of revelers.

She said, "I'm not a very happy person, Clay. Couldn't we just talk somewhere?"

He was like a little boy offered his first candy bar.

It was off season and he usually spent the time with his parents, but he got away on the pretense of a week-long fishing trip in Alaska.

They met in a motel in Seattle, the Holiday's off-season home, and while he came prepared to answer her need for someone to talk with, the handshake greeting soon escalated into some touching. And some all-over kissing, then they were shedding their clothes, and Clay, the 27-year old for whom sex was some heavy petting in college, was being taught what the real thing was all about by this gorgeous, insatiable siren.

She said, "Clay, I think I love you for more than your pitching."

They discussed the futility of the liaison. It really wasn't love. They knew next to nothing about each other. She was in her second marriage and needed more attention than the always-busy Matt Holiday could provide.

She said, "He tries, but he just isn't with me enough, Clay. "I can't live with that."

Clay decided she was going to have to. The off -season sessions had been a delight, but the meetings were difficult to arrange during the season. Holiday traveled, often with the team, and he was busy with other out-of-town errands including scouting and league matters. Matt Holiday would be a candidate for league president one day.

Clay was becoming a better know figure in Chicago, so they had to be careful. On two occasions, in late mornings after night games, Clay took a suburban Burlington train to LaGrange, the town just east of Hinsdale, and walked to the Holiday house.

Then Clay met and began his string of dates with Naomi. Sissy was curious more than angry when she and Matt ran into him leaving the Toddy House with a blonde on his arm. She got him on his cell.

"So what's the story?"

He said, "Her name is Naomi Stafford. She works for Canfield, for your husband, in fact."

"Is it serious?"

No, but we've had several dates. At least I can be seen in public with her."

That stung. "I want to see you. Soon."

Clay wanted that, too. They had to face it, talk it out, but the affair had to end.

Allen Cookson called with a suggestion for communications counsel and Clay met with Warren Omeara, president of Omeara and Bleeker in New York during a Yankee series.

He told Omeara, "I want to speak out against the Beach scheme. I also want to run ads in every major city. So big they will get attention. Television, too. I'm writing them now. I know what needs to be said, and I have some material for you right now and I'll write more on the plane going home. What will it cost?"

Omeara said, "It could run into millions."

"Okay, no problem. I'll tell my agent to release the money as needed. Please schedule the ads for immediate release."

In his apartment two days later he found an unaddressed envelope taped to his mailbox with a terse message. It said, "6:30 Palmer House bar," and the date, three days hence. No signature. Sissy would have known of the team's off day.

He would keep the date, but he had to finish his copy for the ads, and put Omeara in touch with his agent, Hugh Jensen. How Sissy arranged for the delivery of the plastic key for Palmer House room 429 he would never learn, but he would be there for their last date.

Naomi kept in touch with Beach by email and cell phone. She found writing and personally placing the meeting ads enjoyable. Kirsten set up the sessions. It occurred to Naomi that Kirsten and Beach might be lovers but as she had no personal interest in the man, she didn't dwell on the matter.

The second week on the new job she had a new associate who introduced himself by tele-phone.

"Brian Strang. Pam Kirsten wanted you to meet me. I'm a Chicago coordinator for OSON. I move around town promoting the idea. Want to go to a ball game?"

The abrupt invitation made Naomi laugh. But what the hell. She hadn't had anything like a date since the split with Clay.

She wasn't surprised he was African American. She was resigned to working with Blacks as be part of the OSON experience. The movement could hardly have a White man roaming Black neighborhoods promoting the OSON idea.

Strang was tall with a strong athletic build, light-skinned, Black hair with a curl. She was impressed with the smile, huge and lit up by excellent teeth. He picked her up at her apartment in a cab which they kept for the drive to Cellular field. They were barely underway before he startled her.

"Pam said you've had a bad experience with Black people. I hope I can help ease your fears."

"Wow, you don't waste much time in describing your mission."

"Pamela, Beach, too, consider it important that your view of African Americans be as objective as possible. I guess I'm the first Black male you've been this close to in your entire life."

"That's probably right. So what?"

"I might quote Shakespeare. Didn't one of his characters say something like, "Prick me and do I not bleed?""

"It went something like that, but most White women aren't concerned about mixing words with educated Black men. They fear violation, pain, and even death."

"Yeah, see what you mean. You infer I'm educated . Partly. I have a law degree out of DePaul. Jeremiah Constable sold me on the OSON program. I have about two thousand prospects for the new community. Our New York agent has twice that number, and we're making progress in other major cities as we pick up more coordinators. OSON is paying me seventy-five thousand a year. How are you doin?"

Naomi didn't mind admitting she and Beach hadn't discussed a salary. She had no worries about money , but was surprised with the amount of the check she received a few days after her last meeting with her new employer.

"I'm gainfully employed by the Canfield group. They own the White Sox."

"I know that, but you might as well get on the gravy train. Mr. Beach is loaded. I admire the man. If anyone can make the idea work, he's the man."

The game was fun. And made more dramatic because Clay Burnside was pitching for the Sox against the Detroit Tigers who were nipping at their heels for first place in the American League's Midwest division. Strang led her to reserved seats on the third base line, close enough to recognize Sox players as they moved in and out of the dugout, but high enough so they could get a good view of the action.

She declined Strang's offer of a beer, but she shared some peanuts he shelled and dropped into her lap.

He chatted almost constantly about the action on the field. She knew only the basics of the game. Nine innings. Three outs and teams changed sides.

Strang said, "Clay has his A-game going tonight. The slider is unhittable and he's mixing in the other stuff beautifully."

"How do you know so much about the game?"

"I was a prospect once. Typical story, hurt my arm. Just as well. Very few make the big leagues. My high school coach was also a lawyer and encouraged me to get serious about school. Worked out okay. Can I get you a coke? How about a hotdog?"

Naomi thought, "If Beach and Constable can find more people like this guy, their the idea has a chance."

Clay had shut out the Tigers through six innings and the Sox had a run. Naomi was surprised when he was replaced. "Why did they do that?"

"He probably could go on, but they don't want to wear him out. Besides, they have good middle relief and closers."

Which proved correct. The White Sox hung on to win the one-run game. Brian grabbed her arm and they hurried down an escalator for a cab. He invited her to eat something, but she said she was tired. He dropped her at the curb before her apartment building, making no move to accompany her to the door. but waited until it closed behind her. He told her later he didn't want to scare her by lingering, as if for a kiss.

"She said, "Thank you. I had a great time."

"I'm glad. We'll do it again." And he was gone.

30

"Your ads are doing a great job." Beach told Naomi in a call from a meeting city,

We have good audiences everywhere, but I don't want that task to be the limit of your creativity. Have you thought about coming with OSON full time? We need to set you up in an office."

She enjoyed the praise. She said, "I'm ready to resign. I'll make it formal with a note to my boss and make the switch to coincide with your return."

"Good. We'll be back in Chicago in a week and you can start looking for a permanent office."

It was a Monday morning over coffee when she was startled to learn she was a "person of interest" in the Burnside murder case. A regular reader of Sid Coffin's "Summing Up" column, she read the writer's tribute to Clay based on his long distance talk with the pitcher's father. The encomium ended with, "Clay Burnside was as innocent as newly fallen snow, but your columnist has learned of his meetings with 'two blondes' The depth of the involvement is unknown, but CPD's Sergeant Leo Carey hopes that someone might come forward to help the identity at least one of these ladies."

Her first thought was, "Why haven't I been picked up? Surely someone saw me with Clay. Or had they? It was only a three-week relation-ship, with a half-dozen dates. They would meet at some public place away from the Cellular office or he would pick her up at her apart-ment. One of their meeting places was the Toddy House where they saw but did not speak to Matt Holiday and his wife as they left the bar. This fleeting glimpse must have been the source of Coffin's news about Clay and a blonde.

They were not together at the Holiday party and she wasn't in any of Clay's photos. So what to do?

She would try to contact this Sergeant Carey, the officer mentioned by Coffin. It was the right thing to do and if it helped lead the police to another "blonde," so much the better.

Or should she? Would the publicity put her in a spotlight she didn't need, possibly infringe on her efforts for OSON. Adele had cautioned her about rash decisions.

"Remember the awful deal in buying your first car."

She would sleep on it, but it would be wonderful if she could help find Clay's killer. It was tragic his ideals and her bigotry, or fear, broke up what might have become very special.

31

Leo Carey was stumped, and he was very unhappy about it. Even granddad Damon couldn't ease his frustration for being at a dead end on a case he wanted to close so badly.

Damon said, "Something will happen to help you, Leo. You've been in this spot before."

"Yeah granddad, I know, but this one is so special. That fine young man, and his beautiful parents. I have to close this one or I'm going to quit, maybe go private where I can bend the law now and then to get the bad guys."

In his last session with Bob Henry they had gone over their interviews with both men and women guests at the Holiday party.

Henry said, "It looks like a dead end with the Holiday guests. Except for the Sox people none of them had any connection with the man, They hardly knew anything more than his name and that he was a great pitcher.

"He was a private guy, with more brain power than most of his mates. He came to games on time, worked out per the schedule he designed with the trainer, Ed Phelps, and went to the hill every five days."

Leo said, "Well, I'm going call Holiday about a meeting with the entire team, coaches and staff. I still think someone knows something that will help. Maybe having them all together will jar something loose.

"At least we know how the killers got into the hotel. Al Durkin swears that no one on the kitchen staff was involved. He didn't like to admit the kitchen people leave the back door open so they can duck out for smokes, but they do. The kitchen was very busy at that time, cooks with their pots and pans and waiters rushing in an out. I can see how a couple of guys could get past with-out being noticed."

"Bradshaw is on my ass about working out. I'm going to do some push ups and other stuff, then lunch at the Bear. Meet me there."

Leo did an honest work out, but sighed at the scale after showering. The needle hovered at 1. It was going to be a light lunch.

Restaurateur Baiano was not a cheerful greeter. "It's Louis, he's missing, for two days."

"Why didn't you call me?"

"He's gone missing before, but only for a few hours. It must have to do with the gambling."

"Who takes his action?"

"I'm not sure, but I can find out."

"Do that. Can you still make me a hamburger?"

"Of course. Man, I had to do a lot of short order before I owned a restaurant."

Corrine worked late, so he had no one to chat with. He ate his hamburger slowly, going over the same items as he had reviewed for the last several days.

He used his cell to call Carole.

"Hey, Get out a BOLO for the Bear cook, Louis Laporte. White, about five-ten, hundred and fifty. His boss, Sal Baiano, said he's been missing two days, but he's in hock on some bets. He drives a ten-year old White Ford Focus. I expect have something on who takes his action in a hour or so."

Henry walked in.

"I got a call from outfielder Larry Craft. He said he ducked into the locker room for a leak a couple of days before Clay was killed and saw him hang up his cell in a hurry. Might mean something if we could find the cell."

"Yeah, the killers leave his wallet un- touched, but take his phone. We have another mystery. Sal's cook is missing. He's in hock, gambling. Sal thinks he might be in deep. I hope we don't find him in a park lagoon.. You go ahead and order something. Sal just gave me the eye. He may have a contact for us."

Sal had news and he was worried.

"He was in for around ten thousand with a hard ass type named Gino Valetti. I know of this guy, but haven't had direct contact. He is known to be an impatient bastard, wants his money but won't just have people beat up. They disappear. He must be a mean son of a bitch if he won't give people a full chance to pay."

"Yeah, I've heard of him. Former New York mob guy. He's been questioned about a couple of missing people, but lawyered out of charges or came up with alibis. I have a lot on my plate, right now, Sally, but I'll check this one out personally."

"Oh thank you, Leo. How was the sandwich, okay?

"Yes, you haven't lost your touch around a grill. Now give me a check. I'm buying for Henry."

Naomi was sure the police would want to interview Holiday party guests. It took her only a few minute on her computer to break into and erase her name from the list computerized by Matt Holiday's administrative assistant.

After sleeping on whether to make herself known to the police she decided to make the call. *It might help. I might get my name in the paper, but so what.*

She found a number for the police department and told the voice that answered that she had some information on the Burnside murder.

"Hold, please," A few seconds later, a voice sounding as if it came from a large man, said, "This is Sergeant Leo Carey. Who is this, please?"

"My name is Naomi Stafford. I may be one of the blondes you are looking for. I read about the search for blonde women in Sid Coffin's column."

"I would like very much to meet you, Ms. Stafford. Can I pick you up? I'll buy the coffee."

Oops, she didn't want a police car showing up at the office.

"I'm busy at my office right now. Could you meet me later at my apartment on the near north side." She added the address before he could object.

"I sure want to meet you, Miz Stafford, but I understand your problem, What time will work for you?"

"Let's make it five thirty. I'll wait in the lobby."

"Okay, but give me a phone number. In case of a mix up."

She gave him her cell and they hung up.

Leo called Henry. "Bob, I just got a call from a woman who thinks she is one of our blondes. A Naomi Stafford. I can't see her at her apartment on Ogden until five thirty. You can go out with me if you are available."

"Hell yes, I'm available."

Leo was still frustrated. It looked like it would be a long day of watch watching. He should have talked Stafford into an earlier meeting.

Then, as it happens in police work, when there's a break in the turmoil, something always comes up. Carole had bad news.

"They found Sal's cook, half dead. A good Samaritan was walking past the Bear alley where two thugs were pounding on the poor guy. He called 911. The thugs ran for it. Louis is in Michael Reese, but unconscious. The EM doctor said they hope they can bring him around for questions."

"Okay, I'm going to the hospital. Tell Henry to meet me at Stafford's apartment."

Laporte was still in the emergency room when Leo arrived. The pair of officers who brought him to the hospital were standing by to give Leo a report.

"Any chance we'll be able to talk with him?"

"The doctors aren't very optimistic. Do you want us to hang around?"

"No, go back on duty. I have a couple of hours of free time. I'll stick around on the chance he comes out of it."

Leo had never felt comfortable in hospitals. There was always the fear of being a patient, lying there helpless, unable to move. He remembered the hot summer evening when he covered a domestic dispute with fellow rookie Bill Kelly. They were just about to climb the fourth flight of stairs in the west side apartment building when a White male, in his thirties, who had left his wife unconscious in their apartment kitchen, stood on the landing waving a pistol. He was looking down at them, obviously drunk, and when Bill held out his hands in the by-the-book appeal to calm down, and said, "Hey man, take it easy," the man fired twice, hitting Kelly flush in his chest protector.

Leo caught Kelly as he fell back and dragged him out of the shooter's sight. He pulled his thirty-eight.38 service revolver and laid it on the floor alongside the unconscious officer. The academy had covered first aide for shock. His first move was to call dispatch. He didn't yell into his shoulder phone. Neither did he use code other than to identify himself as a cop.

He said, "Officer down, needs paramedics." He gave the address, then worked to remove Kelly's jacket and the ballistics vest. He was breathing, thank God. He wouldn't have to use AR. He propped Kelly's jacket under his head.

A couple of hallway doors opened with only heads emerging. He ordered, "Police business. Stay in your apartments."

The dispatcher would send back up along with the ambulance, but Leo wanted to have the scene under control. He picked up his revolver and went back to the stairs.

He yelled, "Throw down the gun. If you have it when my back-up gets here you are as good as dead."

A defense attorney learning Leo's threat might have tried to charge Leo and the CPD with using an illegal tactic to force the easy surrender, but the shooter wasn't versed in the law. The heavy .45mm automatic bounced down the stairs, preceding the contrite gun slinger. The incident earned Leo one of his many citations.

Leo felt the need to talk with someone. He found a found a nurse who looked as if she had some authority.

She was Maureen Hamilton, already deep into overtime. He told her who he was and that he was going to stick around with the hope of learning more about who beat up on his favorite cook.

The tired nurse didn't care to chat. She said, "Good luck" and went about her business.

He called Sid Coffin on the reporter's cell and got a one-ring pickup.

"What's up big man?"

"I might be a little late tonight. Will that be okay?"

"We can wait. Will you bring me some news?"

"I'll try. Bye."

33

The good-looking young woman was seated in the lobby of her near north side apartment as promised.

Leo stepped in front of her with a smile.

"I've been looking for a special blonde. I hope you are the lady."

Naomi couldn't respond to the officer's good nature. She didn't have a smile in her.

"Yes, officer, I believe I am. My name again is Naomi Stafford, and I enjoyed a brief

friendship with Clay Burnside."

Henry came in and they were alone in the lobby. Leo saw no need to find another place for the interview. He and Henry pulled up a chair to sit opposite her.

"Please tell me about this friendship?"

She had rehearsed her remarks and didn't hesitate in taking it from the top. She described the dates and their nature, almost day by day. She closed with, "I would have come forward sooner, but I only heard the two-blonde story in Sid Coffin's column."

Leo thought, "Thank God my buddy has all those readers."

"But you didn't see him several days before he died. Why was this?"

She was ready. "I made a remark that he construed as racially based. He is, was, a very intense young man about racial matters. He said nothing, but he didn't call me again."

Leo didn't ask the obvious question. He doubted whether she used the N word, but it was probably something related.

After all the years in law enforcement he still hated to ask his next question.

"Did you have anything to do with Clay's murder, Ms. Stafford?"

"Of course not. I was very disappointed in the breakup, and I was stunned by the news of his death. I hope that something I say here, or at least that I came forward, can help you solve this case."

"How are you employed, Miz Stafford?"

She brightened slightly. "Coincidentally, I work for the Canfield corporation. I manage the office for Mark Holiday, the Sox general mana-ger."

"Didn't you attend Holiday's big party? I don't remember seeing you in any of Burnside's party pictures, and I don't believe your name was on the guest list."

She told him how she erased her name.

"It was dumb. I think I felt unwanted, and just decided to dis-appear. I'm truly sorry if I held up the investigation."

You sure did, kiddo, but at least we've cleared up the 'two blonde' matter.

34

It was always fun meeting with Sid and his lovely wife, Marian. It wasn't long ago the marriage was in trouble, imperiled by Sid's loose behavior during his often all-night forays for columnar news. Marian's forgiveness became part of a wild finish as Sid and Leo found themselves in the office basement of Chicago alderman Paul Petrovich. What happened then was the basis for Sid's summing- up story, "The Byline Murders."

Sid had a question as he brought Leo his beer.

"Anything for me on Burnside?"

"Well, our search has been reduced by one."

Leo described his meeting with Stafford. "It's coincidental she works for the Sox. Matt Holiday met her, but it never occurred to him she might be one of our blondes."

"He's been distracted."

"You could say that."

The rest of Leo's visit was spent in the pleasure of Marian's roast. Leo couldn't resist a second serving.

Marian mostly listened to the men. She was a White Sox fan and lamented the death of her favorite pitcher. She was up on the story, having read Tribune coverage as well as her husband's column.

She said, "How in the world did he agree to that hotel room? There could have been a dozen better places for a tryst."

Leo said, "Her scheme may have suited him because he thought she had taken so much care in booking the room. He was satisfied no one would spot him."

"Oh yes," she agreed.

Sid said, "I still smell gamblers, but Clay would have brushed them off and reported contact as required. He was a multi-millionaire. Who could buy him? I suppose he could have been threatened."

Leo said, "I never met the young man, but I heard the story of his life from his father. That plus what we've learned about him to date has convinced me he was unapproachable by anyone trying to set up something.

"Which reminds me." He smiled at Marian.

"My next favorite cook is in the EM at Michael Reese. I'm going to make a stop and see if he woke up from the beating he got from a pair of gambler's goons."

At the door Leo grabbed his friend's hand.

"I owe you for the introduction to Stafford.

Now maybe you can help us get blonde two."

Sid said, "If she's blonde. The woman in the bar who followed Clay to his room, the woman your witness saw in the hallway. What the hell. She could be a red head."

Leo again took the outer drive to his side of town, turning into the side street that led him to the hospital He could have called to learn of Laporte's condition, but he wasn't ready to hang it up for the day.

The desk at the EM told him the cook was still unconscious but had been transferred to critical care. He called dispatch. Nothing for him. He went home, turned on the TV for late news and hit the sack.

Preston Beach was back in town and if a mature super wealthy business mogul can bubble with enthusiasm, it was the leader of OSON.

He told Naomi over the phone, "It's going to be a movement. Our coordinators in Los Angeles, San Francisco, Portland, and Seattle are doing great jobs. Eastern and major Midwest points are on board. Can you get away?"

Naomi checked her list of to dos. Holiday was with the team in Pittsburgh. There was nothing on tap. She returned Beach's call and agreed to lunch in his Ambassador suite.

Constable, all smiles, met her at the door. Lunch had already been delivered. Beach stood with Constable and Kirsten as Beach introduced a short, bald, middle-age Black man.

"Naomi, meet Homer Carrington of Carrington public relations. Mr. Carrington came in from New York to coordinate our first press conference. We'll have it here, in Chicago, It's time, the word is out. With the major west coast cities on board we can utilize all major news outlets to tell our story completely and correctly."

They sat around the room with their plates of food as the wound-up Beach talked.

"I've never been more enthused over our chances for complete and immediate success, well in advance of original plans. And your excellent work in advertising our meetings accounts for a major part of my enthusiasm, Naomi.

He nodded at Carrington. "Would you bring Naomi up to date on your plans. Homer?"

The stocky man was not convivial. She thought he might be a little full of himself, but she was soon assured he was a complete professional.

He said, "Chicago, with its large Black population, is perfect for our first big break out.

Preston, you and Jeremiah have done a great job in cementing contact with major Chicago-based thought leaders. Several of them will join you at our press conference the day after tomorrow. We'll have no difficulty getting out everyone from your local dailies to the Wall Street Journal and the Associated Press. Television will be well represented and we will have our own coverage.

"Press packets are about ready. As you know, Preston, they will contain your personal background data as well as the complete OSON story. We still have time to include pix and quotes from some of your major contacts around the nation."

He took a breath, and to Naomi's surprise, smiled. "That's about it. If you don't mind I'll head over to my Chicago office to supervise things there."

He was on his feet, and walked to the door. Beach and Constable walked with him.

Carrington paused at the door. "I should remind you of the anger White Sox pitcher, Clay Burnside, has for OSON. I've heard he has hired a competitor of mine, Omeara public relations, and he may buy a broad media attack. He can afford it."

Beach said, "I think we can weather almost anything."

Pam Kirsten hadn't uttered a word through all this. She now smiled at Naomi.

"Whew! Are things moving along here, or what?"

Naomi had spoken to Beach's close aide a number of times during their western tour, but she was impressed with what now seemed her associate's humanity.

She said, "Whew is right. That Carrington is a little power-house."

"Yes, he has worked on major political campaigns, including presidential. Not only is he our counsel, but Preston has convinced him OSON is the way to go. Preston hired him over the phone after checking with the Public Relations Society of America. He didn't know the man was Black, a real bonus."

Naomi was wondering about her future activities with the campaign. She thought it might be important she get set up in an office as Beach had mentioned,

Preston confirmed the idea.

"We need to set up a Chicago office with you in charge, Naomi. Carrington is on full time and you will coordinate his efforts after the press conference. Weren't you impressed with him."

"Yes, I just exchanged whews with Pamela. It's a nice coincidence he is Black."

"Right, he is involved in other Black-related do-good stuff. He's in perfect position to help us approach Black professionals, intellectuals, and educational leaders."

"How about the BAGA?"

"Good question. Carrington is a member of their board. How about that?"

Naomi could understand the man's buoyant mood.

"Okay, I'll give notice."

"Good. Jeremiah s already on the hunt for downtown office space. I'm tired of working out of hotel rooms."

"Me, too," said Kirsten. She exchanged a quick look with Beach.

"That's it, they're lovers,"

Beach was at the suite's desk, writing something. He strode to her smiling, holding out a check.

"An about-due bonus, Naomi. Also, you're expense account for anything related to OSON is unlimited."

She said, "Thank you! You are very generous and I'll try to earn all this."

"You will, don't worry. You will think the world has fallen on you after the press meeting. Hey, we forgot to drink our champagne. Jerry, will you pour."

36

Naomi and Constable talked on the phone about the best location for the OSON offices and agreed to meet at a real estate firm of his choice.

She then called Adele, reported the bonus bonanza and that day's meeting with Beach.

Her mother's lingering doubts had been put aside, but she had another worry.

"Honey, I think you are involved in a movement, all right, but now, I'm going to worry about your physical safety. Neither the Black nor White worlds are going to be completely in favor of your OSON."

Naomi felt secure enough, but she asked Constable about safety for OSON people when he picked her up the next morning for the office hunt.

In his car he said, "There have been no incidents among our regional associates. We have little to fear from zealots, Black or White. The drug people shouldn't see OSON as a problem. We won't interfere with their filthy trade. In the states, that is. As for the White bigots, the basic "back to Africa" crowd, they're all for us."

They met with a representatives from Warner Bertram Real Estate who described several downtown locations, then drove them to two on north Michigan. Naomi approved both of them, but favored the one on Grand across from the Drake hotel. "Where we can deposit special visitors. It's also an easy cab ride for me. I can see lots of late hours.

"There are offices for you, Preston, and Kirsten, which with all your travel won't be used all that much. The reception area looks okay, and there's space for my staff. Right now I'll need a secretary-assistant and a filer, but there's room for more. I vote for making a deal."

Constable agreed. The lease papers were made ready as Naomi and Constable talked about how she would look for her aides. He did the signing for OSON then taxied to the Ambassador. She used one for her return to her Cellular office where she would break her departure news to Holiday who was back in town.

He was in his office and incredulous from her news. He had read her resignation note, and wanted to know why she would leave "a job you are doing so well."

She saw no harm in describing her new job. and tried to give him the basics.

"Holy cow! OSON, huh? What's it all about?"

Naomi had been standing in front of his desk, hoping it would be a brief meeting, but she had his attention. She should try to clarify her reason for joining the Beach movement. She pulled a chair in front of his desk and quickly described Preston Beach and outlined his goals.

"I'll admit to a fear of Black people, made worse after the rape of a close friend, but I now have a more realistic understanding of the Black situation in America. I believe OSON offers American Blacks a much better opportunity for better and happier lives in their own world."

Holiday was trying to make sense of what this bright and good looking young woman was getting into.

"As I see the picture your OSON will invite Blacks who are already successful, or at least are functioning okay, to leave us with all the dregs including a huge prison population. I don't see how it will work because America and other democratic nations are based on private enterprise and competition. You're describing a utopia, where the good life is offered on a silver platter. It sounds like the communistic ideal which didn't work in Russia, or Cuba. It doesn't work because some people want more of the pie, I, for instance, want to be a Walter Konenberger,"

Naomi saw where he was coming from. It was the basic posture of Americans who had achieved status they believed came from their own efforts, and good luck. They ignored or forgot the help from their families and other connections, including the educations they had been given.

Holiday must be aware that huge number of current college graduates, Black and White, are mired in debt without little hope for jobs in their chosen fields.

She would not argue with him. He made an important point. If Blacks buying into OSON thought they would be able to lay back on their American achievements, and not strive to excel in their new African nation, they might create a harmful inertia. She left with a handshake.

Holiday shook his head. "You are young and idealistic, Naomi. I hope OSON works. I know you will do all you can to make it work."

"Thank you, Matt, and good luck with the team. I'll miss being close to the action."

37

Leo was on his way to check on Louis Laporte's condition, when he got Sal Baiano's call.

"He's awake and alert, Leo. Are you going to see him?"

"I'm on the way, but thanks for the call."

Bob Henry was on his second morning cup of coffee. Did he want to accompany Leo?

"Sure."

They found the cook smiling up at nurse Maureen Hamilton who was taking his vitals. She seemed much more at ease than when Leo met her in the emergency room.

"He's doing fine, despite the bandages," Hamilton said. "We're shifting him to general population this afternoon."

Leo said, "Good to see you, man. Now what can you tell us about the goons who put you here?"

"Damn little, Leo. Never saw them before, but the one who hit me the most had an arm full of tattoos. I remember a heart with a stake through it, that's all."

Leo said, "Sal told us you were in pretty deep. Ten thousand. Did the goons say anything about the money you owed?

"No, they must have been told where I was hiding out. With my sister. They grabbed me when I was going out for some beer. They hauled me into an alley and started hitting. Oh, it hurt. I think they wanted to kill me."

Henry said, "Who has been taking your action?"

"A little Black guy called Mouse. He lives somewhere in the neighborhood. And another guy called Dutch. I never would have got away laying off that much with just two guys.   I was dumb. I told them I was good, but I was into everything, baseball, football, college and NBA basketball. It got out of control."

Leo said, "I've seen the one called Mouse a couple of times in the Bear. Okay, you get well, but your gambling days are over. You understand that?"

Laporte's look was that of a kid whose hand got caught in his mother's purse,

"Yeah, I know I gotta problem. I'm done."

In the car, Henry said, "I hope he's done. It's a hard monkey to get off your back."

"Yeah. But in his case, it might be a life or death decision. And he's not off the hook yet. We are going to have to protect him until we can find those scumbags. Look, I'm trying to set up the team meeting. Why don't you try to find the guys LaPorte mentioned. Maybe Sal can help."

"Sure. Drop me at my office. I'll look up a snitch who's into horses."

Carole had nothing special for Leo. She rang Matt Holiday for him.

"Matt, Leo Carey. I need a favor. I'd like to talk to the team. All together. Coaches, trainers, the works. Can that be arranged?"

"Of course. We're home. I'll set it up before tonight's game. Everyone is in the club-house by four. Make it then."

"Thank you. And Matt, will you be there, too. It would help impress the team if you were in the room."

"Sure."

Henry called "Leo. I got the Mouse. He said Laporte was into him for eight of the ten gees but he heard of no orders to beat him up. Sal thinks he can help us find Dutch, so I'll stay with it."

"Okay, and it would be nice if we can find who those people report to."

Leo spent the rest of the morning working on the talk he would give in the Sox locker room.

He was convinced someone might have something that would furnish a lead on why Clay Burnside was murdered so brutally.

He drove over to the Bear for lunch. Sal greeted him.

"I gave Henry a couple of names he might talk to. I have a sub cook. What'll you have?"

"Something light. I'm going to work out this afternoon."

He settled for chicken soup and a ham and cheese on rye.

He waited another hour before going into the gym. He was greeted by a half dozen men, most of whom needed weight loss more than he did. He worked hard with sit ups and pushups. The sweat poured, along with a few ounces of suet, he hoped.

He showered and shaved. He wanted to appear a fit and ready cop when he met with the Sox group. He didn't bother to use the scale.

He was wearing his best beige sports coat and a pair of new loafers. He thought he would walk to the ball park as part of his workout.

A guard at the player entrance admitted him without hesitation. Holiday had alerted the elderly man, Eddie Burke, who had a twenty-five year reputation for guarding the door from those who shouldn't go through it.

He said, "Come on in, Sergeant."

Leo pulled his notes from a pocket as he walked up a ramp to the locker room. It was a few minutes to four but the room was crowded. The players were in various stage of dress, or undress. When Holiday came out of Grimes's office, the room quieted quickly.

Holiday introduced him.

"Fellows, you may have heard of Sergeant Leo Carey. He has been involved, and in fact solved, several prominent cases over his career. I know we all want him to solve the case that has horrified us all. Sergeant Carey, you're on."

"Thank you, Matt. As a way of seeking common ground with you men, you might be interested to know I played baseball on the ground now supporting this new stadium. I cannot say that I shared your level of talent. You have a great team, and it adds to the Clay Burnside tragedy that his loss threatens your hopes for another championship.

"I've come to you today in the hope that you may have heard, or possibly witnessed, something that may have impact on our investigation."

Leo raised his voice. "Larry Craft, are you here?"

Craft, still in his civilian clothes, stepped from the rear of the room.

Leo said, "In a talk with my associate, Bob Henry, you said you saw Burnside on a phone call which ended when he saw you come into the clubhouse. Would you mind repeating what you saw on the chance it might provoke something from other players or coaches."

"Sure, Sergeant. I remember it very well.

The entire team was on the field. I ducked in to use the toilet and saw Clay on his cell. He was hunched over as if he didn't want to be overheard and hung up as soon as he spotted me. I didn't hear a word he said, but he obviously didn't want me to hear him. I gave it no further thought until I remembered and called officer Henry."

Manager Grimes spoke up. "As we all know, Clay was a quiet man, did his speaking from the mound, but it seems to me he was acting preoccupied about the time of the call Larry described."

Another voice from the rear of the room. It was catcher Luke Ordwell.

"I asked him if he had any plans for after the game. I wanted to talk to him about the Indian lineup he was going against in a couple of days, but he turned me down. Said he had other plans. I kidded him. 'With a woman,' I said. He actually turned red."

That was going to be it. No one else had anything to contribute. Leo thanked the group, and Holiday and Grimes. He turned to leave the way he came in. "I walked over from my office," he explained.

There was a tug on his sleeve as he left the room. It was coach Shorty Cox.

"Probably doesn't mean anything, but I think Clay was seeing someone. About a week before he was killed, a day game, I had an errand and left as soon as I could change. But Clay beat me out the door and climbed into a cab with a woman. I couldn't identify her, but I think she was blonde."

 Leo could put Shorty's mind at rest.

"Yeah, Mr. Cox, it was a woman we have identified, but I appreciate your telling me.

Cox was tearful "I really loved that boy."

Leo hurried to the player entrance.

God almighty, I have to solve this case!

Leo spent the evening with Damon. They chatted while watching some pre-season pro football.

Damon said, "It's too bad your victim wasn't a guy who threw his weight around, leaving possible suspects all over the place."

"Yeah, Clay was one of the quiet ones. He may have had something going with a woman I interviewed, but she said the romance went on the rocks when she said something racial."

"Oh yeah?"

"Yeah, Clay is, was, very anti-bigot. We found a thank you note for a generous check he sent one of the Black support groups. The woman I interviewed is very intelligent, and cultured. I don't think she used the N word, but something upset him so badly he broke off the relationship.

"That was too bad."

"Yeah, too bad."

38

Pam Kirsten had reserved a large public room in the Hilton on Michigan for the conference, and Homer Carrington got the turnout he predicted.

He was very modest about it. He whispered to Naomi, "Preston is one of the most important business leaders in America,. We even have financial editors out there, but we won't pass out the kits until he winds it up."

Cameras from all three networks were set up, along with those from CNN and other independents. A double-wide lectern was jammed with microphones and call letters.

Naomi thought, "I don't think the president could get better coverage."

Kirsten handled Beach's introduction, much as she had introduced him in Chicago and other major cities. He was not unheard of, nor was OSON, but media coverage to date had been spotty.

She thought he looked rested, and calm. He smiled and led off with his usual strong voice, thanking his audience for turning out, then adding, "I hope you find my remarks newsworthy."

Naomi was standing alongside Carrington. His head jerked and she thought his face showed a grimace. He later told her, "The remark was unnecessary. Of course what he said was news-worthy. It's how news-worthy that counts."

Beach did follow Carrington's counsel in

keeping it short, stressing main points. He took it from the top, but only covering the main OSON goals and his optimism for achieving them. In their pre-conference meeting Carrington stressed brevity.

"Your answers to questions will fill out your OSON story and the press kit will cover every-thing else."

Almost every hand was up . Naomi thought the flood of questions was much the same as asked by Mrs. Wilkins, and others at that memorable first meeting with Preston and OSON.

Beach appeared to welcome them all, even those openly dubious of the idea.

He said, "OSON has a movement, as real and powerful as lava spilled from a volcano. Within five years we will have transported a cadre of more than twenty thousand Black Americans to Africa. In ten years a half million.

"The complete ten-year plan is described in the kits you will be given at the end of our meeting. Are there more questions?"

Walter Jones of the Independent, a Black-owned Chicago daily identified himself and asked, "Will there be a free and independent media?"

"Of course, and if you like, your affiliate will be the first established. A television station and AM and FM radio stations will begin as soon as our citizens create readers and an audience."   Carrington was right when he said it would be a long session, easing up as reporters phoned editors and recording and camera equipment were packed up. Some print people hung around hoping to get additional quotes. Tony Bacon of the Associated Press told Carrington his bulletin would be followed with chunks from local press coverage. Coffin overheard Bacon.

"Why don't you write it yourself?"

He enjoyed twitting AP staffers who regularly borrowed from member's proofs.

"Ah Sid, you guys write so well,"

Carrington who had worked the room with several aides from his Chicago office, came back to Naomi.

He said, "The Wall Street Journal will call Preston for an exclusive this afternoon.   The Reuters stringer told me he would have a major. story. That means coverage around the world. That includes Africa, of course."

Naomi congratulated Carrington and told Pam she would not return to the suite with her.

"I'm going to the new office and interview some applicants. See you later if I'm needed."

Naomi interviewed a half dozen prospects, hiring as aide and secretary an Amanda Jenkins, a Black graduate of the University of Illinois, Chicago branch, who said she was bored with secretarial work in a legal firm's pool. She had heard of OSON from a young man, name forgotten, who had spoken about the movement in her church.

"The young man wouldn't have been Brian Strang?"

"Yes, you know him?"

"Sure. He's our Chicago coordinator. Good guy. Took me to a ball game."

"Well, I should say."

39

Leo thought he could "deduce" as good as any detective, and he enjoyed reading the adventures of Sherwood Holmes and the more current sleuths, but like most cops it was nice having a snitch or two who could furnish a helping hand.

He was standing with one in the alley alongside the Bear hoping to learn the whereabouts of Dutch, the other LaPorte bookie. The contact, an alcoholic named "Red," had just offered the opinion that Dutch might be dead.

"Valetti is pissed that they let Laporte get in so deep. I haven't seen Dutch for a couple of weeks. I don't have any idea where he might be holed up. It's big town, Leo."

It was unproductive, as most such meetings were, but Leo still reached for his wallet. He would give Red the minimum sawbuck.

Red had snatched the bill, and was turning away when they heard a screech from up the alley, near the restaurant's back door. In the darkness of the alley three men were struggling. One of them was Louis Laporte.

Leo's first thought was that the goons who had injured Louis so badly were back for another shot. But how did they get into the Bear kitchen? Sal had a gun, but Leo was to learn later the owner was not in the restaurant when the thugs walked in.

They brushed past Corrine and another server and burst through the kitchen door.

What the hell! Leo grabbed for his Magnum. He wasn't going to shoot unless he had to. He might hit the cook, but he was going to use the heavy gun to fight off the thugs.

He was into the squirming trio in a couple of seconds. He got his left hand into the collar of thug one, yanked hard and swung his heavy automatic into the back of the man's head. Down he went, pulling Louis and the second thug down with him. Leo then stabbed his gun into the face of a surprised hoodlum.

"Let go or I blow your head off."

He told Phelan it may have been the easiest pinch of his career.

"There I was, standing in the alley next to my CI, and these idiots grab Louis."

Ted Serbo answered his call for back up and drove the hoods to lockup. One was barely conscious, the other screaming for a lawyer.

Serbo told Leo, "The clown said they were only going to talk to LaPorte. You got to them before they started any rough stuff."

Louis said they were the same pair that put him in the hospital.

"I thank God you were there, Leo. What a break it was for me."

Phelan wondered if they would deal for a reduced sentence, but Leo doubted whether they would give up their boss, presumably Gino Valetti or one of his people.

"They'll try for a deal," meaning with someone from the DA's office. "They're both losers and don't want to go back to jail, but Valetti might go after them wherever they are."

"I'm going to talk to the hood. Just to warn him to leave Laporte alone."

The boss gambler wasn't hard to find. Sal Baiano came up with an address, in Cicero of all places, Al Capone's last stand.

Leo invited Henry to drive out with him. They talked Sox base-ball. The team had lost two straight and was falling back in the closing days of what was expected to be a championship season. With Clay Burnside, that is.

"I've never been as discouraged as a cop," Leo said. He pounded his hand on the dash.

Henry sighed. "It's a bitch. Maybe we might learn something today. Clay was a straight arrow, but there might be some connection."

The address on Randolph street was a bar. They parked in a lot next door. It was mid-after-noon. Only four or five cars were present. Leo wondered if Valetti would be available.

He was. There were several mid-day customers and a single bartender. Alongside the bar was a closed door. Leo did not explain his mission. He let Henry flash credentials while he pushed the door open to a long narrow room in which several men sat at a round table. They had interrupted a card game.

Leo said, "I'm Sergeant Leo Carey, CPD, looking for a Gino Valetti."

He was facing the bulkiest of the men he judged to be all Italian Americas. He was also the spokesperson.

He said, "You found him, officer, but aren't you out of your jurisdiction?"

The voice had no ethnic accent, and he was smiling . He moved a hand as if dismissing his companions. That's what he meant. The four other men stood as one and walked into the bar.

Leo guessed he might be of medium height. He was clean shaven, with a full head of jet black hair. He was in white shirt sleeves with a red and blue designed tie loosened slightly. A suit coat was draped over the back of his chair.

Leo said, "Yeah, Mr. Valetti, I guess we are, but we came to talk, not arrest anyone."

"Oh, what should we talk about?"

"It's about a compulsive gambler, a cook in my favorite restaurant, who I believe is into you for ten thousand dollars. His name is Louis Laporte and he was beaten, almost to death. He recovered and was back on the job when two goons tried to repeat the assault, but they were apprehended before doing any damage this time. and are in Cook county jail."

Valetti made a small grimace. "That's good

to hear, I mean Mr. Laporte's recovery and escape, but I know no such man."

No surprise, but the disclaimer set him up for Leo's message.

"You are known as a gambler, Mr. Valetti, and we expect you to get the word out that Mr. Laporte is strictly off limits. He is not to be contacted on this matter, in any way.

"In the meantime he is going to raise and pay one half of his debt. That would be five thousand dollars. This is going to be the right number to get him off the hook. You, or whoever he owes, are going to absorb the other five thousand as a business loss. It's my personal slant, but I think gambling bosses should be able to recognize clients who are hooked and slow to cover their losses. Laporte doesn't make a lot of money, so it's going to take awhile, but I have his assurance he will pay off his debt. You should know, too, that he is no longer a gambler."

Valetti's look was thoughtful.

"I'm impressed that you, Sergeant Carey, would step in this way. I've heard of you, read news reports of your successful police work. I read Coffin's column, too. You must be a special friend of the reporter.

"Tell you what. I'm not really a gambler. I own this bar and have a few other interests, but I'll make an effort to get the word out. It's hands off Mr. Laporte who must be a very good cook to have earned your protection."

For a moment Leo thought he might reach for the man's hand. Driving home, he told Henry of the urge, quickly put down.

"The man's a murderous son of a bitch, partly educated, the worst kind."

40

Hugh Jensen mourned Clay Burnside's death for more than the pitcher's ability to make the agent a rich man.

He told his wife, Mary, "The man was the classiest athlete on the continent. A gentleman who had room in his heart for every other human being."

Clay had rushed Jensen copy for both news-paper and television messages. Jensen called Warren Omeara and worked out the plan for financing and placing the full-page attacks.

Jensen told his client, "Man, this is powerful stuff. It might border on libel."

Clay said, "I don't think so, Hugh. I read up on libel and slander in college. There may be a question about malice, but I'm clearly speaking my mind which I know is the truth. If we go to court and I'm found guilty you will just have to get me a contract that will pay them off."

They laughed together over that possibility.

It was ground zero for the campaign. Clay was dead, but the ads would begin the following morning. The copy was explosive, and Clay, helped by BAGA research, had some favorable governmental numbers.

He told the agent, "Hugh, we'll blast Beach and his OSON right back where he came from, into his business world."

Those were the last words Jensen heard spoken by Clay Burnside, but he was cheered by the certainty the pitcher's attack ads would be devastating to the Beach movement.

41

Naomi was jolted awake by her mother's call.

"Naomi, grab your newspaper. Clay Burnside is speaking from his grave."

Naomi grabbed her robe, then pulled the Tribune off the floor in front of her door. She spun through the pages. She knew Adele wasn't referring to normal coverage. She gasped when she saw the full large-print page with a headshot of Clay at the top.

The headline in huge type read, "OSON Attacks Black America With Unworkable Scheme."

Oh my God! She read it all, then took more time for a reread. The man she thought she could love let it all hang out in a denunciation of Preston and his big idea.

He wrote, "The dream that African Americans play a successful role in America is taking place now. That they have to be transported into a communistic-socialist culture to find fulfillment is preposterous."

She dressed hurriedly and cabbed to the office, meeting Amanda Jenkins at the door. Her aide's look said she might have seen the Clay ad, but she didn't say.

Within the hour the office's bank of phones was ablaze. The calls were from New York, Boston, Washington, and other cities along the eastern seaboard. Naomi had hired only one other aide, Betty Booth, a recent grad from Roosevelt, Naomi scrambled between calls to instruct the two women on how to respond.

"Keep cool. Tell them the Burnside attack is unjustified, and might be libelous. Also, they can be assured Mr. Beach will respond quickly."

The trio struggled for an hour, then calls from the Midwest began. Fortunately Brian Strang and one of his volunteers came in to help man the phones.

Brian said, "Your response is good Naomi. I got to Constable, and he will be here soon. Preston will take calls we relay to his suite."

It was a rough morning with no respite. Naomi tried for a laugh. "We'll all be hearing bells in our sleep."

Amanda sent out for lunch.

Preston reached Brian on his cell, wanted to know how it was going.

"We're buried, and it will get heavier when the west coast comes in. Ma Bell is making a ton."

Beach wanted to speak with Naomi.

"How are you holding up?"

"It's been a workout."

"Brian said you worked up the right response. Nice going. You've read the man's ad, I presume."

"Yes. Fallacious might be the word for it."

"Right. We'll fight back with the truth.

Unfortunately the young man has a lot of cash. Carrington knows the agency that handled the ads. He's using TV, too."

"Wow!"

"Wow is right. We are fighting a man who is famous for his baseball, but he is out of the picture. His murder is a tragedy, but we have time on our side. It heals all wounds, per the adage, and we will prevail. The Black Americans we want will agree with us, and we will maintain the support of the White America that counts. Is Jeremiah there yet?"

"He just walked in."

"Put him on, please, and thanks again for your good work."

Naomi finished the day, and night, in a daze.

The team stayed on until midnight, bringing in more food. The west coast calls were pretty much the same as the rest. Callers knew Clay Burnside.

His successful career began in San Francisco.

The questions were all over the place. Callers identified themselves as Black, White, Latin, and Asian, Some questions were intelligent, and articulate. Other callers rambled. One woman asked whether Burnside might be a White-appearing Black person.

Finally back in her apartment, she got out of sweat-soaked clothes and made some coffee. She doubted whether it would keep her awake.

Too late to call Adele. She sank into bed, trying to think it out. Clay, that beautiful, idealistic boy-man. He was no loony. How sad it was that they couldn't have found some common ground for agreement. He just smiled and walked out of her life.

Was he right? He had two basic points to his argument. First, he charged that the basic idea of a new nation for Blacks was ridiculous, that problem confronting the idea were insurmountable. Then he wrote that Black America was deep in talent, that subs would easily move up and fill the vacated spots. He said schools were brimming with talent, with graduates in medicine and law along with MBAs in business and finance anxious to move into the White society success-fully. He included numbers that seemed to back him up.

She told Beach the words were "fallacious," but was Clay's argument really deceptive, or misleading per the definition of the word?

Maybe she was giving the boss what he wanted to hear, "kissing ass," per the office vulgarity. In any event she would try to earn her generous salary.

Adele called. She had seen the TV version of the Burnside attack.

"Too bad he couldn't have delivered the words himself, in the television version, but it was still a powerful argument."

"Mom, whose side are you on?"

" I'm always on your side, honey, but your father and I want you to be on the right side. You'll remember, I was dubious of Mr. Beach, but you convinced me he had a good idea. I do want to be objective, and the baseball player seem realistic in his objections. I hope you can sort it out. We don't want you to be caught in the middle."

At the office, it was more of the same, but not the deluge of calls of the day before. Amanda and Betty appeared to be on top of the situation.

Amanda said, "Most of the calls are from people who saw the television spots."

Naomi knew baseball players salaries in a general way and Sox wages in particular. They were up in the millions for the stars, and Clay was a super star. He approved the raid on his bank account for this effort. She could visualize him pouring over his pages of copy, and she had no doubt he wrote every word.

She wondered about his youth, upbringing, and education. What had turned him on to the hopes and needs of Black Americans? He must have grown up with Black kids and loved those friends and teammates as he developed as an athlete.

Her life experience was completely different from Clay's. She sat alongside Black college classmates, said hello, but never met them. There were no challenges to her basic racial attitudes. She wasn't a "hater," but the shock of her friend's attack crippled her ability to see racial matters objectively.

The therapy that helped return her to society and hold a job made possible her initial curiosity and introduction to Beach and Constable.

Clay was a superb human being and his passion for his beliefs would probably hurt OSON, but what had become love for the man would not shake her belief it could work.

Her reverie was interrupted by Brian Strang who suggested lunch. The volume of calls had eased, and they found a restaurant on nearby Grand avenue. She ordered a salad with ice tea. He asked for a ham on rye and skim milk.

"Skim? You're worried about your weight?"

"Not really, but I'm going to lay off fats, caffeine, too. I've been into a dozen coffees a day and it's making me jumpy. I see you have a disciplined diet."

She said, "I agree about the caffeine, but I do love my ice tea. What do you think so far? About our OSON situation?"

She saw his hesitation and understood. He had no idea how close she was to Beach.

She said, "I'm not a spy, Brian. I'm with the program, but I also dated Clay Burnside for a few weeks. I'm trying for an objective view, but still stay loyal to my employer."

He said, "So am I. Right now I think we have a stand-off. As a semi-educated Black man I like the idea of living free from the so-called 'White oppression,' and I agree with the ball-player that I could move up in a United States grown short of successful Blacks who have left for the new world.

"At the same time, I might be well placed in OSON's new nation. Hell, I might become a judge in Africa."

They both smiled at the inference. She enjoyed the company of this very good-looking young man. The ball game "date" had been fun and now felt completely comfortable with him.

She said, "You can become a judge here. I think you might have a tendency to put yourself down."

"Well I haven't seen a lot of opportunity to put myself up."

He made her laugh with that crack.

They ate their food in silence, but she thought he might be looking her over as she had him. Would he propose another date? Something other than a baseball game?

They walked back to the office. It was a great September day in Chicago. A slight breeze tugged at her skirt and bathed her legs. She was smiling. Brian saw it and hoped she was happy. She was. Right now she was enjoying the pleasure of being a good-looking American woman.

Beach was in the office Naomi had set up or him. He stood at the door and beckoned for her and Brian to join him. He had also invited Constable and Kirsten..

He said, "I just want you key people to know I haven't taken a step back in my plans for OSON as a result of the Burnside attack. It will subside. He was a very wealthy young man and apparently left a huge portion of it for his misguided campaign, but it will end, and we will move on successfully.

"I've decided we will not fight fire with fire. Carrington suggests an ad campaign of much smaller but well-placed messages that support our stepped-up meeting campaign. Jeremiah and I will make television appearances both in teevee spots and as an interviewees. Carrington suggests a film, too, for distribution to clubs such as Rotary, Elks, and the like. It would show our African property, and some of the bull-dozers already in action. We can out spend and outlast the Burnside campaign. Brian, you and your fellow coordinators have a big job. You've done well, but will need to exert even more pressure to unite Chicago's OSON community."

"Yes sir."

"Naomi, your job is as critical. Work with Carrington to plan our return visits to cities that need special help"

Naomi nodded. *The energy of the man.*

He said, "Our position is still solid. Burnside cites colleges and other training sources to fill the holes left by OSON's recruitment, but he's wrong. The raw talent just isn't there, and I doubt whether a government that can't make decisions on other important matters will wake up to realize the crisis.

"Americas has to do a much better job educating its children. Most politicians regard the idea of free college educations as impossibly expensive. Free advanced education will be part of our plan. I have to remember to emphasize that point in future talks."

Kirsten spoke up. "I won't let you forget."

"And we should emphasis our commitment to the climate change crisis."

Beach led the group out of the room and took a phone from Betty Bloom's hand.

"Hi, this Preston Beach. Do you have a question or comment on OSON?"

Naomi shook her head in admiration.

Whatever happens this man will be the last man standing.

42

Leo had another question for Naomi Stafford, and tried to reach her at her Cellular office. He was told she was not longer a Canfield employee. He identified himself and got the name of Stafford's new employer and phone number.

He couldn't get through with a couple of tries. He gave up and turned the effort over to Carole.

Her efforts took several tries, but finally someone picked up and told her Stafford would return his call.

Sid Coffin called.

"Have you read Clay Burnside's attack on OSON? It's sensational. Read it. It's a full page. We'll talk later."

He hung up.

Leo hadn't read anything but sports for the past several days. He had brought the Trib with him that morning and shuffled through it, easily finding the page with the huge headline.

God, the young man was angry. Leo shook his head over the emotion that jumped off the page. Clay's father said his son had strong feelings on the matter. He read the tirade twice. He wasn't so much surprised with Clay's position on behalf of Black America as he was impressed with the skill he presented his argument. The words jibed with what had learned about Clay from his father and Naomi Stafford.

But why in hell should Stafford take a job with that outfit?. She has no love for Black people and if a huge population of successful, law abiding Blacks were going to emigrate she would have even more to worry about.

Carole said, "She's on."

"Thanks for returning my call, Miz Stafford. I have a question, but I was surprised to learn you've joined this OSON thing. You had a friendship going with Clay Burnside that broke up over something you said he regarded as anti-Black. I can't help but be curious about your new role."

She thought, "It really is none of your business, officer," but she said, "I attended an OSON meeting and thought Mr. Beach has an interesting idea. I later met with him and his key people. I was satisfied with their explanation of the total plan so I signed up."

Leo wasn't going to press the matter.

She has to be pissed at my nosing into her business, but if it has something to do with Clay's murder, it is my business.

Naomi wasn't all that surprised with the detectives show of interest in her new post. She was after all still a person of interest.

She said, "You'll remember I immediately regretted my outburst that last date, and I was very disappointed when he dumped me. Have you read his attack ad?"

"Oh yeah. He made some good points.

"Yes, he did, but I'm committed to the OSON movement and I intend to see it through. You had another question?"

He grinned. *This is one bright young lady.*

"Clay had a cell phone. Any idea what might have happened to it?"

"No, I can't help. He never used a phone while he was with me. How would it help?" Pause. "Excuse me. Of course it would help. It might lead to blonde two. Right."

"Right, and that's all I have for you, Miz. Stafford. I think Clay's death hit you hard. I wish you luck in whatever you do."

"Thank you, Sergeant. Call me again if I can be of any help."

Leo left the conversation with more curiosity over OSON. He should learn more about what set off Clay Burnside's explosive reaction.

"Carole!"

He asked her to learn when and where there would be another local OSON meeting.

It took her a couple of minutes.
"Fort Dearborn hotel. Eight tonight. "

43

Leo ate at the Bear about seven to allow himself plenty of time to get downtown. Corrine was busy, but she made an effort to say hello.

"What kind of day did you have?"

"Uneventful, but there's still a chance some-thing useful might happen. How about you?"

She rested her hip on the table. He thought it added to the profile with the rest of the curves.

"I audited that psyc professor again. He talked about disciplining kids. What would you do if your three-year old boy ran into the street in front of a bus?"

"Well, I'd try to grab him, of course."

"I mean after?"

"I'd probably hug him to pieces."

"The prof said that's not what you should do. He said you should give him a shake and scold him. That would register more than the hugs."

"I'll try to remember that."

She moved on and he thought, "It would be nice to have a child again, but what kind of a dad can a twenty-four seven cop make?"

Sal Baiano walked by and Leo looked up from his T-bone. "How's Louis holding up as a non gambler?"

"He's itchy. I'm taking fifty out of his check every week. You sure those guys will be patient?"

"Yeah, I think so. If Valetti isn't directly involved, he knows who is. He doesn't want me coming down on him."

Leo left twenty per cent on his tab this time and resolved that would be standard with Corrine. He drove the outer drive downtown on the crisp September evening. It promised to be interesting. Preston Beach was sure to refer to the Clay Burn-side attack as part of his spiel.

He was surprised to see Sid Coffin in the hotel lobby.

"Hey man, what's up?"

"I'm interested, same as you, in how Beach will respond to Burnside's attack."

"Yeah, you haven't written a thing since your coverage at the press conference."

"Right, but it's my third OSON meeting and I'm about to become my opinionated self."

Leo patted his friends arm. "As a loyal reader I'll be as usual interested in your views."

They found a pair of seats in the rapidly filling room. Pamela Kirsten stepped to the lectern and introduced herself , then said, "Mr. Beach has asked me to introduce tonight's program with reference to the horror with which we at OSON learned of the murder of White Sox pitcher Clay

Burnside. Many of you have read or otherwise learned of Mr. Burnside's attack on the OSON plan. Because Mr. Beach must now respond to Mr. Burnside's objections he wants you to know his heart is out to Clay's family and friends, his teammates, and to the world of sports."

Beach stepped into her place.

"Thank you, Pamela."

To Leo, the man didn't look as if he was anxious to leap into a subject he had presented and defended many times. He had asked his aide to describe his feeling about the murder, but he couldn't leave it at that.

He has to respond to the attack in every speech he makes from here on out.

He glanced at Sid whose eyes were frozen on the speaker.

Beach spoke softly. He needed the amplification of the mike attached to the lectern.

He began, "Clay Burnside and I share, or shared, an ideal; that is, to help every African American fulfill dreams to become a successful American. Unfortunately this is not possible in our current culture. In the vernacular the cards are simply stacked against the average Black child, and their frustration continues through the rest of their lives.

"Mr. Burnside represented the best possible example of our American middle class. I have learned he was reared in a family that encouraged both his involvement in scholarship and sports where he teamed with Black and Latin athletes who returned his friendship and support.

"He backed his belief in the progress of Black America with active participation in BAGA and most recently with his declarations in his widely distributed attacks against OSON.

"I maintain the young man was incorrect in his belief that a migration of many of America's more successful Blacks would result in their replacement by new waves of Blacks just waiting in the wings, so to speak. It would be wonderful if it were true. We would have the America that would fulfill the goals of our democracy, but in reality the replacements for departing Blacks would likely be mostly White. Tragically, that's how the current America works. Unless we adopt radical changes in how we as a nation regard our Black population and convert a system of charitable support to total involvement in raising the educational standards for every Black child, I see no improvement.

"Now let me devote the rest of this meeting to OSON, its goals, and how we expect to achieve them." Leo thought Beach then turned on the enthusiasm he must have shown in his campaign around the country, and the words that made a believer out of Naomi Stafford.

Beach ended his talk describing what he saw as a new danger to America.

"It's a wave of anti-Black and anti-Semitism that can tear America apart. OSON will have nothing to do with the so-called White nationalism. Along with the hate is the violent opposition to anything having to do with curbing the sale of guns, particularly multi-bullet guns that have no other use than to kill human beings."

Beach then offered post meeting refreshments, along with his availability to talk further with individuals.

Leo might have introduced himself to the man. Obviously Beach and his organization were persons of interest although Clay was killed before his attack ads were aired and published.

It could wait. Right now he preferred the exclusive company of Sid.

He said, "Sid, let's drink coffee, or do you have to go to work?"

"Yeah, let's have a cup. I've already filed a piece for tomorrow."

They found the hotel's coffee shop still open. In a booth Leo said, "Y'know, as I sat there through the talk and questions, I had a normal cop thought. Could the billionaire have anything to do with Clay Burnside's murder?"

Sid sat for several seconds considering his friend's speculation. He nodded.

"Of course he has to be regarded as one of your persons of interest, but the horse was out of the barn. The ads ran after the boy was slaughtered. Beach doesn't look like the vengeful type to me. Why would he make himself an obvious suspect, even if he had advance knowledge of Burnside's attack.

"The pitcher's ads could put a crimp in Beach's plan, but it's had years in the making. His press conference and release material described a huge amount of work to this point. He has already had detractors although nothing as powerful as the Burnside's effort. The young man could really write."

Leo nodded his approval several times during his friend's speech.

"Yeah, but he could have ordered the hit because it would have stopped the kid from writing more. And Burnside could have used the off season to hold meeting just like Beach's."

They sat heads over their coffee. They both pointed to their cups as an exhausted female server asked if they wanted refills.

Leo said, "He paints a pretty bleak picture of America without the Blacks he'll take to Africa."

Sid smiled. "Yeah, that's especially interesting. I'm beginning to wonder if Mr. Beach isn't a one-of-a-kind patriot. He may be hoping that America will respond to his OSON by making new or stronger efforts to elevate Black Americans, dumping the generations of charitable support that isn't working, and substitute educational and other programs that will move more Blacks solidly into our middle class, He knows it will take time and he thinks his new nation in Africa will be a success by then. He may be as much an idealist in his way was as Burnside was in his.

"But I don't see how I can report it that way. Right now, anyway.

"It gets down to who do you believe, the man with huge resources, or the young idealistic dreamer who sees the Black culture as already taking a better place in our society. His writings amount to charging Preston Beach with being a dangerous obstructionist."

Leo said, "Okay, you are going to work. I'm going to call it a night. We still have one blonde, or whatever the color, to go. Why can't we have an easy villain like Paul Petrovich to go after?"

"Right. "

Leo thought how good it was to have become Sid's friend and how they took the crooked politician down, He supposed Sid felt the same way.

Leo was upbeat. The Sox had pulled one out in the ninth. They were still in the Midwest race, trailing the Tigers by two and still close in the wildcard standings.

He had slept well despite the over-supply of coffee. He read Sid's column. The writer said he had filed something other than OSON material, but as usual it was interesting, something about how classical music was having a positive effect in county mental institutions.

It was mid morning when he picked up the call from Matt Holiday. After the usual swap of greetings and Leo's congratulations for last night's Sox win, Holiday said, "Can you get away, Sergeant. I mean could you come out here?"

Of course. Leo called Henry and they drove the interstate to the Holiday home in Hinsdale. An unsmiling Holiday met them at the door. He ushered them into a large library, then left them alone. He did not suggest coffee or anything else. The detectives glanced at each other with raised eye brows. This definitely looked like something other than a social call.

Holiday returned, trailed by his wife in a dark silk dressing gown. Neither Leo nor Henry had met the woman. She was reported to be very beautiful. The long Black hair fell around a pinched White face with little or no makeup. Her eyes had obviously held and released a flood of tears.

Leo thought, "Here is a very unhappy lady."

They took seats in a semi circle. Holiday led off:

"Detectives, Mrs. Holiday stunned me the news you are about to hear. I'm sorry it has been so long in forthcoming. Sissy, will you tell the officers what you told me."

Over the years Leo tried for cop calm in the presence of women in distress. And to stay alert. There was a woman still holding her husband's gun after she shot him. Another woman, who looked in control when he arrested her brute husband, exploded and tried to scratch his eyes out.

He was seated in a comfortable stuffed chair, but still felt the need to shift his large body. He glanced at Henry who was transfixed by the lady. She was obviously not at her best, but he later told Leo, "I thought she was drop-dead gorgeous."

Sissy Holiday had never had to apologize for anything or explain her actions to anyone. She was a firm believer in the quote, "Never explain, never complain."

Why not? She had been a beautiful baby and had become a beautiful woman. There had been a period in her life when she thought she repelled men with her looks. Few boys in high school thought her approachable. She rejected the few who were overly optimistic about making a "score." Other less aggressive boys felt uncomfortable as escorts and the idea of having sex with the creature was for fantasy time. This created a painful level of frustration with her. In college she sat is classes with boys she would have enjoyed meeting and spending time with, but the only invitations came by way of "fix ups" by friends and sorority sisters who really didn't care whether the match ups worked.

She married a man her parents found for her, a wealthy New York elitist who was not all that impressed with her beauty. He was a "switch hitter," who enjoyed the company of a fellow polo player and also dallied with women in their social set. She recognized her hopeless marital situation when she found him naked in a bathroom with their gardener.

Matt Holiday was an escapee from the elite life. His parents paid for his undergraduate degree at Chicago and at Columbia where he earned an MBA in finance. He was a junior executive in Walter Konenberger's empire, rising quickly because of his intelligence and zeal for work. He loved baseball, played it in college, and when he asked for an assignment in the company's baseball division he was sent to a White Sox minor league affilate as an assistant general manager.

After moving up to higher ranked teams he got the major league job by requesting a meeting with Konenberger in his Philadelphia office.

Konenberger told partners. "Hell, this young man is a dynamo. I was aware he produced three straight winners at our double and triple A clubs, but he told me part of the reason his teams did so well is because he had players who weren't given ample opportunity to play at the next level. And he came in with the numbers."

Matt discovered Sissy at a Christmas party for homeless kids. She found refuge in "do good" activities and she thought the handsome baseball executive was a kind and considerate man who was clearly interested in her. After he declared his desire to marry, they indulged in pre-marital sex with the enthusiasm that Sissy discovered she had missed very much, Her new husband proved loyal and tried to share her sexual needs, but he was a busy man, traveled a great deal, and often left her in a bed filled only with fantasies.

She was clearly the aggressor with Clay Burnside. The innocent man was stunned with the attention from this beauty and the affair lasted several months after the World Series victory by Matt's White Sox. He and the team were the toast of Chicago and she felt more loneliness when Matt spent many out-of-town nights the following year rooting for his team. He even enjoyed scouting prospects and visiting Sox minor league teams.

She knew Matt was loyal to her and she shuddered when thinking he might learn of the affair. It had to end. She found a way to arrange a Palmer House room for what she knew would be a last Burnside "date."

She looked downward as she began her story.

"I am the other blonde you have been looking for. I chose the Palmer House because I have never been in it. I thought there was sure to be a lot of traffic in the lobby, and I was confident I wouldn't be recognized if I wore a wig. I used Matt's home computer to work out the room reservation for Clay,

"I knew nothing about the thugs who somehow learned of the meeting and killed that poor boy. I told Matt because I can't live with the picture of Clay lying torn apart in that hotel room."

The officers sat unmoving as she described her need for a last tryst with the equally guilt-ridden lover.

"We knew it was over, but he agreed to a final meeting."

Leo's eyes were locked on her face. Holiday was staring at the wall behind her head. Henry's eyes joined Carey's on the beautiful but tragic face, his mouth slightly ajar.

Leo asked the first question.

"Mrs. Holiday, repeat please how you left the envelope at the apartment mail box."

"I had no key, so I taped the envelope to the metal. It was a desperate move, but I made the delivery in the morning before he might be expected to check his box."

Leo withheld the question as to why she didn't try to arrange the meeting by phone.

She was afraid he would have refused the invitation.. She wanted one last chance to get him into a big bed.

"You must have been seen by the killers. You didn't see anyone?"

"No. I got in my car and drove home. I didn't think anyone noticed me."

Leo then excused himself to take Henry aside for some quick instruction. Henry left the room, tugging for his cell.

The lady was clearly cried out. Her husband sat eyes on the floor. There was no more to be asked or said. He rose and walked to the door with Leo. They shook hands, but it was not a so long with smiles.

Holiday returned to Sissy's side. He knew his next move was to call his lawyer. He had no idea as to the extent of her culpability. He was still stunned over her revelation. He loved her. He was hurt, but it wasn't all her fault. Obviously, he had to reassess his role as a husband.

Leo and his fellow officer didn't talk much on their way into Chicago. They shared the hope Henry's call from the Holiday home would lead to a major clue. The envelope Sissy Holiday used to summon Clay Burnside might be found and pro-vide a recognizable finger print other than Sissy's or Burnside's. Did he still have it when he slipped into the Palmer House that night, and if he had it, did he toss it into one of the room's waste baskets? Or was it in his apart-ment's basket? Saving the contents of all the baskets was a no brainer. Anything Sharp or his aides found in them would have been labeled and stored in the evidence room.

Henry was not happy with what they had learned at the Holidays.

"Do we have to let the DA in on this?"

"Nope. She screwed the boy, didn't murder him."

"How about Phelan?"

"Yeah, I'll tell him, although all we have is a reason for Burnside being in the hotel, which we had anyway. Now we know who he was with."

"Yeah, poor Holiday. Do you think he'll kick the beautiful lady out?"

"Your guess is as good as mine. I don't think she's a slut. She and Clay Burnside discovered each other and it became a train wreck. I hope she and Matt will survive together."

Carole Olson could keep her cool as well as any person in the squad room , but she almost yelled into the car phone, "Leo, they found a small white envelope in the Burnside evidence basket. It's on its way to Forensics."

Leo squeezed the steering wheel.

"Jesus, why didn't you call?"

"I was afraid you'd drive off the road."

Bullshit, but he grinned.

Maybe neatnick Clay Burnside had helped contribute something that might solve his murder.

Leo could feel sweat gathering around his neck. In the squad room he headed directly to Phelan's office with his news from Hinsdale. He was passing Bradshaw's office when he decided to let the Lieutenant in on the possible break. Why not?

Bradshaw liked the formality of a telephone summons, but he looked up and smiled at Leo's invitation. Both men clapped when Leo described what could be a major break.

Leo said, "They're putting a rush on it."

He then delivered the rest of his news. The meeting with Sissy Holiday.

Phelan said, "How about that. What a shocker for Matt Holiday."

Bradshaw said, "She could go to jail,"

Phelan said he had met the lady.

"An absolutely awesome female. Was there a lawyer at this meeting?"

"No, Matt was in shock himself, but I'm sure he will get one now. The man must be hoping his wife has contributed something important to solving this case. He still is the GM of a contender, wants to move on with his job.

"Whatever, we have to hope the envelope gives us a print we can work with."

Elmer Sharp brought joy to the Chicago police department late that afternoon.

"The envelope was handled by several persons, but we found a readable thumb at the corner of the envelope where it was pulled off the mail box. We're asking the national data bank for help in sorting it out. May take a couple days."

Leo told Phelan. "Don't know how I can wait."

Phelan said, "It's been a long pull. I know you never wanted to solve a case as much as this one. Let's go over everything again, from finding the poor kid in 429."

Leo reviewed all that had gone before, from discovering the mangled body to finally coming up with the identity of blonde two and the painful session with Sissy Holiday.

"Thank God she couldn't live with her role in the mess."

He decided to open up the obvious based last night's talk with Sid.

"It's Beach. No one could want Burnside out of the way more, He must know he's a POI. I could bring him in, but we would need another interrogation room to hold all the lawyers."

That made Phelan grin.

"Well, you could still talk to the man, maybe over coffee or a drink."

Back in his office, he picked his phone for a call from Coffin.

"Pal, per our speculating over all that coffee, I've done some research on Preston Beach including a talk with a buddy at the Kansas City Star. Beach owns an auto parts plant in a Kansas City suburb. There was a recent strike. Goons were brought in to break it up. Two workers were badly injured. A guy arrested for leading the scabs and doing the most damages with a bat was a thirty-year old named James Remeau. My friend said his name stuck with him because he was lawyered out by a prominent local attorney.

"Lots of ill will in the split community. The plant is being moved to another location.

"How about that. So he isn't squeaky clean."

"Nope, the explanation given for shifting the plant is that it will be closer to the auto plants they serve. As if a few hundred miles made any difference. The man knows how to run his businesses, but he could have used some public relations in this case."

"Yeah, thanks for digging that up. Now I'll update you on what Henry and I heard this morning. I'm going to ask you to sit on it until we get more."

He repeated the gist of Sissy's confession.

Coffin wailed, "Hey, I can't win this one. You're going to call a conference regardless of what you learn from the envelope."

"No, we're going to sit on it. And I want you to sit on it, too. It could help save a marriage. Just tell your readers we have found the second blonde. I won't call a conference unless we get something usable from the envelope. That may take a couple of days."

"Okay, pal. Get lucky" Coffin had to go along. He couldn't risk doing anything to harm the long and successful relationship with Leo.

Naomi had another date with Brian. They attended a Chicago symphony concert and had a late dinner. She thought she would dress up and wore a new body-hugging black silk crepe dress with pearls for her neck.

Maybe he guessed she go would formal. He wore a gray light-weight flannel suit with a conservative blue silk tie.

He picked her up in his BMW and his eyes showed appreciation for her effort.

"Wow!"

She said, "Wow, right back. You didn't need to dress up."

He said, "I'm dressing up for Rachmaninoff. I love the man. And talking about dressing up, you are gorgeous."

"Thank you. I heard the composer was unlucky in love."

"Well, you can't have everything. Hey, it's a long concert. Are you sure you can hold off for the food?"

"Sure. How about you?"

"No problem."

He dropped her off at the Michigan entrance to Orchestra Hall, parked and joined her in the crowded lobby within ten minutes.

He said, "It looks like a full house."

He had chosen balcony seats third row center. She thought they were perfect, combining a full view of the players with an ideal position for the sound.

The performance was Rachmaninoff's Second Piano Concerto. Naomi had loved it since childhood . She smiled her pleasure through the familiar passages. At the piano was a female Russian star whose confident command of the famous melodies thrilled her audience. At her side Brian tapped the tempo on a knee soundlessly. She wondered about his cultural heritage, his parents, and their background. So far as she knew he was a lifelong Chicagoan. He had mentioned DePaul university law school. She looked forward to their dinner conversation.

They drank Cokes at intermission, returning to hear some Mussorgsky and Shuman which filled out the concert.

Back in the Brian's BMW she said, "This was such fun. I haven't been in Orchestra Hall in years. Thank you so much, Brian."

"You are welcome. My parents took me to concerts as a kid. I liked the romantics, such as we heard tonight, but didn't care for a lot of heavier stuff, and no chamber music."

They had their late meal at a popular restaurant at the corner of Michigan and Wacker Drive. She worked questions about his youth into the conversation over a house special, ravioli.

He told her about a youth that included a private school education, "Harvard high school on the south-side, then the U of C before DePaul. My dad was and still is a lawyer. He knows and encouraged Obama during Barack's south-side years. Supported his campaign."

How does he feel about OSON?"

"He and mom aren't shocked by my involvement, but they are withholding their opinion about the movement. They read and respect the opinion of Sid Coffin. As you know, Coffin was cautious in his early coverage, He reported Beach's goal after the press conference without opinion."

"Yeah, I wonder whether he will ever cut loose. Today he quoted Leo Carey as finding the second blonde. How about that?"

"Gosh, I missed it. That should have some real impact on solving the case."

"We can hope so."

It was a short drive to her apartment. She wasn't going to invite him to come up, but he gave no sign he expected an invitation. He left the car at the curb and walked her to the door. He held his hand out. She took it to pull him closer, and kissed him lightly on a cheek.

He held her hand for a beat, then said, "Hey, it must have been the music."

She let his partial question hang in the air and disappeared through the doorway.

She had kissed a Black man. What was she doing? Would she go to bed with him next?

47

Matt Holiday called Leo.

"We haven't heard anything from anyone about Sissy's confession and wondered what's up. Our lawyer tells me the DA is probably trying to come up with a charge."

"It's complicated, Matt. I told the DA nothing about our visit. We are certain she had nothing to do with Clay's murder, and her news might help us find the son of a bitch who killed your pitcher. All I can see is that she might be charged with something related to delaying the investigation. In the meantime you should know I'm not revealing what she said to anyone."

Holiday said, "Thank you. Neither of us slept much. I guess we were thinking the morning papers would have it on their front pages. At least I have a ball club to look after, but she is in rotten shape."

"I imagine. I suppose you are considering some kind of psychological help."

"Yes, I want her to come out of this thing whole, Leo. She really is a fine woman. Things just got out of control. I know I'm partly to blame."

Leo had never felt more uncomfortable. He wanted to help this man, but counseling husbands about unfaithful wives was not in his line of work. He said, "If I hear anything from the DA I'll call. You might take a few days off, maybe take Sissy on a trip."

"Good idea, Leo. It doesn't look too good for the team right now. I may be free sooner than I like. Goodbye, my friend, and thanks again for not spilling all you heard from my wife."

Jim Phelan walked in.

"You were on the phone, so they bumped the call from Forensics to me. Ever hear of a James Remeau?"

"Nope."

"Did you know they had the contents of two waste baskets in Burnside's file. Remeau's latent wasn't on anything in the hotel room. The envelope with the print was in Burnside's apartment."

Leo was on his feet. "Holy shit. That's fantastic. We gotta find this guy."

"I've ordered an all points . Remeau has a record. He spent time in our county jail on a mugging charge. He also did some time in Los Angeles for punching out his bar-room boss.

"We'll need mug shots and a last address. I'll get Henry on it. Why don't you see if the FBI has anything on him. They could stretch coverage a bit. This case has been in the public eye long enough to attract their attention."

48

Leo was surprised by a call from Gino Valetti.

"Sergeant, I wanted to let you know that I spread the word on the Louis Laporte matter. There will be no further attacks on your cook, at least by anyone known by me.

"I have been asked to serve as a collector for the money Louis still owes. I hope that will be okay and that you will alert Mr. Baiano of my involvement."

Well put. What the hell. I did promise Louis would make good.

"Okay, I'll call Baiano. He told me he's already skimming from Louis's salary, but it's going to take a long time before your contact gets all his money."

"Oh well, Rome wasn't built in a day."

"Well put, Mr. Velatti. Goodbye, and let's not meet again."

It had been a good morning. Paul Goodman of the FBI's Chicago office said he could help in the Burnside case. They were already involved.

"It was a slow day. I saw your all points. Remeau crossed some state lines. Broke no laws. but he was involved in a strike break involving injuries, Released without charges. We'll find your Remeau. If that's how he is still known."

"Thank you, Paul."

"No problem, Hey, you got a break in finding that latent."

"I'll say, man."

Leo thought he would combine Valetti's message with lunch, but first he went down to the gym for a workout. He did pushups and situps until he worked up a good sweat. He showered and weighed in, wrapped only with a towel. He frowned at the number, still holding at 238, but at least he was holding his own.

He drove to the Bear, saw the owner tending a quiet bar and waved him over to his booth.

He said, "I heard from Valetti this morning, He'll broker the LaPorte deal."

"I hope I can be in business long enough to get this thing paid off."

"How's he doing?"

"I guess you mean is he looking for action. So far as I know, he's clean, but I can't look after him twenty-four seven. At least his former touts aren't hanging around.

"Sid Coffin wrote you found the other blonde. Does that mean you are closing in on a perp as you cops say."

"You won't hear me put it that way, Sally, but we are optimistic."

Baiano had a drinker and went back to his bar where he was subbing. Leo ordered a ham on rye and ice tea. He might have a beer later and chat with Corrine. She might have something new to report from her psyc professor. It was interesting that the university permitted auditing of the classes, but they couldn't expect highly paid educators to spot and report the free education seekers over the tops of their glasses. Besides, an education thief could soak up a lot of knowledge, but get no capital from it. You had to have the degree to claim big salaries and fees. So thought Leo Carey.

It was interesting, though, and he admired Corrine for picking up the free education. He wished he could apply it his police work, the item she relayed about scaring a child into safer behavior for instance. It would be great if he could grab Sal's "perps" and shake them into coughing up some higher ups. He was still smiling about that when he strolled into the office, past a wondering Carole Olson.

49

James Remeau wasn't given that name at birth in Chicago. He was christened Robert James Bodecker and spent most his first ten years in a home for homeless children. He was an attractive child but he seemed most happy in bedeviling other children. As a ten-year old he stole other kid's toys with no intent to enjoy them himself. He would destroy the toy trucks or other play-things, then try to hide the pieces in waste baskets where this evidence of his meanness was easily discovered. He was larger than any of the kids his age, and when his victims reported him he took revenge by punching them in the face.

The home was pleased to release him for adoption to a family named Remeau who thought all this good looking child needed was love mixed with parental discipline. He reacted badly to both, stealing cash from his stepmother's purse, making his two younger stepsisters miserable, and ignoring any effort to meld him into the family culture.

He stole his first car at fifteen, wrecking it and costing his step-father a great deal of money. Soon thereafter he joined a gang of kids in neighborhood house-breaking. He was picked up after a fellow thief named him as the ring leader. Released to his parents, he was told his behavior had to change. He reacted by slugging his step-father. That did it for his family membership. He was again a ward of the state until he was eighteen when he was released with only the warning. "Keep your nose clean."

He was a very large and powerfully built young man at six-three, weighing more than a hard 225 pounds. In the reformatory gym he ignored basketball, but enjoyed seeing his arm muscles bulge from workouts with weights.

He thought California would be a fun place to live, and after a brief Cook County jail term for a botched mugging he worked his way westward at jobs not requiring references. He muscled parts in a junk yard, washed dishes and automobiles, and got fired from a car-parking job after joy riding in an irate owner's Cadillac. At nineteen with an always inner itch to hit someone, he signed up for a Golden Gloves amateur boxing tournament in St. Louis. He did well with a flailing, non- stop attack, until he met a boy with some training who knocked him out in two rounds.

Finally, in California. he joined a forest fire fighting crew and stayed with it for several years, acquiring bartending skills during off time. He was fired for drinking from stock on one of his jobs and did six months in a Los Angeles county jail for punching out his boss. He tried drugs but preferred alcohol. He met and dumped girls he found in bars, and was dumped by several who didn't regard his rough manhandling as love making.

The idea of forming a relationship that might last more than one night never occurred to him. He smashed the nose of one woman who called him a loser, and decided to leave the area rather than face the wrath of her several boy friends.

He was jobless and down to less than a hundred dollars when he drove his ten-year old Ford into the outskirts of Kansas City. He was on the way to his home town, Chicago, where he hoped to somehow connect for a way to get some cash. Taking a full-time job wasn't in his plans.

It was approaching midnight when he turned off the freeway and rolled up to the first bar he saw after leaving the ramp. Several solo drinkers were hunched over their last comforts from their only friend. Remeau found a stool at the end of the bar and signaled for a beer. He was nursing it and staring at the cracked mirror behind the bar when a short, stumpy Latin man slid onto an adjoining stool

"Big man, you look like someone who could use a buddy. Especially one who has an idea on how to make some money. Want to talk about a job I might have for you?"

Remeau acknowledged he was being spoken to only when he heard the word money. He turned only his head to look at the brown-faced runt who had interrupted his plan to rob the place. He was going to wait in the parking lot and strong arm whoever closed up, then raid the cash register.

The Mexican Latin, Alex Ordonez of Los Angeles, was worn out and discouraged after a failed search of several days for a male who had the rough exterior and size of this obvious loner. He waved for a dupe of whatever the big man was drinking, asking himself if the big man was as unhappy as he looked. His late-night visit to the decrepit outpost for lonely alcoholics may not have been wasted.

Ordonez stood to earn his fee and a bonus if he could to organize a gang to break a strike at a suburban auto parts plant. The plant owner, Beachco, a multi-international giant based in the city, wanted the plant back in production in a hurry. Its major customer, a Chevrolet assembler in Texas, was also bleeding cash from the hold up.

For reasons the workers holding the plant wouldn't describe, they refused to negotiate. The agent who contacted Ordonez in California said the matter was urgent and the fee with a possible bonus sounded good. Ordonez had not led a strike for several months. Organizing scabs to break them was his specialty, and this offer found him in a poor cash position. He was not as successful in settling problems with women as he was with workers and roustabouts.

He didn't ask how the Beachco rep found him. In Kansas City he reported to a tall man whose skin was barely a shade lighter than his. He was not given a name when they first met in the back of a tacky restaurant, but the advance payment of $10,000 and the promise of $15,000 more with a bonus if the plant was back in operation within ten days, closed the deal. No handshake. Ordonez knew he had a tough challenge in a strange city. He considered taking off with the down payment, but the Beachco agent found him once and would surely have come after him again.

Sensing he had the big man's attention, and anxious to end two long days and nights of recruiting goons in dumps like this one, he got into to his subject quickly.

"The employees at a plant near here are split in a strike. About a hundred men are holding the place. The workers I represent don't think the strike is going to work and they want their jobs back. There's a couple thousand bucks in it for you if you can get them back into the plant. Five hundred if you show up, and the rest if you get the job done. What do you think?"

He had thrown it out fast. It had been a useless hunt for a strike leader to this point. He only wanted to pay a thousand, his usual starting offer, but maybe an extra grand would wake up this guy.

Remeau was tired, too, but two thousand bucks for his muscle was worth hearing more.

"You want me to go in first?"

"Right. The men you would go against are mostly veteran employees, Family guys. Wave a club and you'd scare hell out of them."

"Is there a gate to break down?"

"No gate."

"All right, but two grand for getting my head busted. You gotta be shitting me."

Ordonez was organizing an action he knew might be adjudged illegal, but the strikers, holding the plant had refused arbitration. If his workers, plus "sympathizers" could take over the plant they could get the work stoppers back to the bargaining table. From his recruitment and scouting thus far he knew the suburban community, a home town for almost all the strikers, was a wreck, split over the discord now three weeks old.

He said, "Well, what do you think the job is worth?"

"I want five. Two before we leave this bar and three after I help your bunch take over."

"That's ridiculous. How do I know you'll show up?"

"The price is now ten."

What the hell did he have to lose? There was a firefighter buddy in Cal who bragged about striking a car plant that was losing a half million a day.

The Mexican recoiled. "Hey, calm down. Give me a chance to think this out. I have to make a call."

He slid off his stool and walked toward the door. Remeau waved for another beer.

Jesus, this son of a bitch is bluffing. I'm gonna make some money and have some fun.

The Mexican, brow furrowed, returned to his stool after the fake call.

"I have approval to pay the five, two if you show up, but you don't get the other three until my workers are definitely in control of the plant. I don't have any money on me. You get the two when you show up on break day the day after tomorrow."

Remeau stared at the man for several seconds.

"Okay, give me a couple hundred for a room and food."

Alex had that much left in his wallet and handed over the money while describing the plant site and when he would meet his fellow scabs and plant workers.

"Get some rest. You can handle it, but there's bad feelings in this town."

Remeau still slept in the car for the few remaining hours before dawn. He found a no- name motel for the eve of the strike break. He used the free day to scout the plant site and rest. He didn't see cops on the site. The Mexican must have put his scab-worker crew together without alerting the law.

On the morning of the break attempt he pulled old work gloves from his car trunk along with a bat. Both items were left over from fire-fighting days, the bat from off-hour softball.

At the strike site, he found about seventy- five men. Only a few of them were in his age range, about half of the others looked like the

Mexican's pickups. The Mexican arrived in a red current model Buick. He motioned the crowd to gather around him.

"Employees, hold up your hands. Okay, you people are officially informed that ending this strike by force may not be legal. The workers keeping you out refuse to negotiate. That is illegal. If you employees join these volunteers in taking the plant back you may be breaking the law, but you will have possession of the plant. The people you're going against know that whoever is holding the property whenever you go back to the table will be in the driver's seat. That means it isn't going to be easy. If you want to drop out, now's the time."

He grabbed Remeau's arm and held it high.

"Here's your point man, He's getting a bonus if he gets you in that front door, so he's going all the way."

Remeau, hyped on several cups of coffee, waved his bat. He punched the shoulder of a man six-inches shorter and twenty-years older than he was and said, "This could be fun."

The would-be strike breaker, his belly hanging over his belt, grinned.

"Okay tough guy, I'm right behind you."

Remeau didn't know what the Mexican was warning the workers about. Legal shit. He had eighteen one-hundred dollar bills in his pocket which he intended to earn. He looked over the opposition, a mass of older men spilling from the plant door, each holding something for the anticipated brawl. To Remeau it looked like pieces of pipe.

He gripped his bat and took his position in front of the recruited workers and his fellow scabs. He thought they all looked scared shitless, but ready to go through the hell to come. He glanced at the Mexican who was moving toward his new looking sedan. If they got in the plant and the Mexican disappeared he would stay in the city, find the son of a bitch and kill him.

"Let's go," he yelled, and led the charge in a fast walk, waving his bat as he neared the first line of defenders.

The melee squeezed a century-worth of pain into only a few minutes of action. Remeau swung his club wildly and was surprised at how quickly the defenders gave way. As he lashed right and left he remembered the Mexican's mention that the plant was filled with veteran employees.

"Family men. Jesus, they are scared of me.

I should have held out for ten.

He felt his club make contact with bodies and heard screams of pain. He took some blows, too, but hunched his shoulders to take the mostly

glancing hits on his back as he waded toward the plant door about fifty feet ahead.

Ordonez had earned his money. He had found the right man and enough "volunteers" to join legitimate employees for the fight. Their youthful leader 's youth, size, and strength made the difference.. He watched from his car as his $5,000 point man swung vicious and damaging blows through his progress to the plant door.

Remeau had thrown the last defender away and reached the plant door when sirens and warning shots were added to the carnage. Cops waded into the melee with their own clubs. He was inside the plant door when a uniform had an arm around his neck and yelled that he was under arrest. He and a dozen strike breakers were pushed into a wagon and hauled away. One cop yelled, "You're going to be charged with causing a riot."

The cop was wrong. None of the strikers was charged. He had no idea who handled their case or whether the strike had been broken, but after a sleepless night he and all the other strike breakers, about half and half company employees and scabs, were told they were free to go.

"Not bad," said a Ordonez recruit who had groaned over his bruises through the night. "I'll hurt awhile, but we got a couple of bonus meals,"

Remeau walked from the cell wondering how much the Mexican paid his scabs, and whether he would get the rest of his money. In the jail lobby he was met by an unsmiling man in an expensive suit who didn't offer his name or hand. He said, "That's it. You've been discharged. Your record is clean in Kansas City."

Remeau was out the door and into bright sunlight when the Mexican stepped from his Buick and took his arm.

"You earned your money, big man. My people got their plant back."

Remeau didn't smile. He should have held out for ten. The fat envelope the Mexican held out fit into his back pocket.

Ordonez said, "When we met you said you were a Chicagoan. I have connections in the windy city. When you get settled in give me a ring. Here's my card."

They shook hands and Remeau held the car door for the Mexican whose name he never learned. Maybe because he never asked for it. There was only a phone number on the card. Remeau glanced at the Buick. The Mexican's lone passenger, a light-skinned Black with a full head of hair, turned away from him.

50

Back in Chicago Remeau found a room in the Hyde park neighborhood near the University of Chicago. He picked up a cheap cell phone and tried the Mexican's number. The answering voice promised a call back.

Several days later it came through.

"How are you big man? I'm calling because I have something that might be of interest to you."

"You want to break another strike?"

"No no. This job is much easier. If you are available I need someone to watch over a Chicago White Sox baseball star, Clay Burnside. Just while he's in the city. I'm paying three hundred a day. It could run into some decent money."

Of course Remeau was available. He had made no effort to find a job. He was planning on something he had wanted to try since California days. He wanted to pull off a heist. Not a bank, He wanted an easier target.

The first night on the Burnside job he sat in his car and watched the pitcher enter his apartment building. He then cruised along 55th looking for a bar, and slowed when he heard music flowing out a place called the Bear.

He was on his second beer when he felt tap on a slightly sore shoulder. A male voice said, "I know you."

The recognition was instantaneous although he had forgotten the name.

"I'm Dick Clements for Christ's sake."

"Oh, yeah, how the fuck are you?"

The exchange of experience since their teens in a Chicago reformatory was somewhat parallel.

Remeau described his western jobs, but didn't mention the jail time or the strike.

Clements said, "I was out east. I found jobs but nothing worth a crap. I heard there might something in Chicago."

Remeau remembered Clements as a kid who knew all the answers, smart in classrooms but kind of a wise guy. He heard one teacher describe him as "bright but lazy."

"You working now," he said.

"Nope. You?"

Remeau described his Burnside assignment. "He's pitching tonight. Why don't you watch the game with me at the bar, then come along when I tail the guy?"

"Sure. Sounds interesting."

Burnside was relieved after allowing a run in six innings. Remeau said, "We'd better go. He might take off before the game's over."

He was unaware that when Burnside pitched and left the game early he showered and waited in the clubhouse until to game's end, to celebrate or commiserate with his teammates. For the White Sox ace it was almost always to savor a victory.

It was a short drive to the ball park. Remeau found a spot outside the player's parking lot where they sat for more than an hour, listening to the end of the game. It was a White Sox victory, but it didn't matter to either of them,

They spotted Burnside in his Black BMW as he drove through the gate with other high-priced models. They followed him to his apartment and were back at the Bear soon after seeing his taillights disappear up his building's parking ramp.

Over his beer Clements said. "I want to stay in Chicago, but I'm running out of cash. There are jobs in plants outside the city, but I hate to give up my apartment."

Remeau said, "Don't do it. If you have room let me move in. I can help with the rent. I'm working on an idea that could flush some real cash. I've been scouting a super market in south shore that takes in thousands from six cashiers and the desk that collects the lottery money. We can be in and out the back door in a couple of minutes."

Clements said, "Could work, but let me think about it. I spent some jail time in Cleveland. I don't want to go back. In the meantime, you are welcome to move into my place."

Remeau was alone the next morning, staked out across the street from Burnside's building, when a Black Lexus sedan pulled up across from the apartment entrance, A slim brunet in black slacks and pink blouse walked quickly to the front door. In one of her hands was a small white envelope. His eyes followed her into the building and lingered on the door. She was back in less than a minute, without the envelope, squinting against the early morning sun.

What the hell. She probably didn't live there. The good looking lady was delivering a message. Maybe to Burnside. He waited until she drove off, then seeing no other persons who might later identify him, he walked into the apartment's postage alcove.

The brunet's envelope, held by Scotch tape, was stark against the bronze boxes, their covers flush against the wall. The envelope was pasted against Burnside's box. Remeau didn't hesitate. He pulled it free carefully. The envelope was barely pasted at its tip.

Holy shit. Her one-sentence note to the ballplayer said was to be with her the next night in the Palmer House's room 429. What the hell, why didn't she wake him up now? He may have been in for a treat.

He replaced the note and envelope. The tape was still fresh enough to hold it in place. He was certain he had welcome news for the Mex. He would call him in an hour. The strike breaker was in another time zone.

Not so. He was in Chicago.

He was obviously pleased about the brunet's note. "Good, that's good. I need to meet with you. Soon."

Remeau said, "Any money in it?"

"Yes, a lot of money."

They met an hour later in a back booth of a Milwaukee avenue restaurant. Remeau ordered a beer. The Mexican waved the server away and didn't speak until Remeau's drink was served.

Remeau said, "How are things in Kansas City?"

"Okay, the plant is operational but the strike caused a lot of resentment on both sides, You did a good job. You waded into those poor guys as if you were having a good time."

"Yeah, I was letting off a lot of steam. Things hadn't been working out so well before we met."

"You aren't on the run, are you?"

"No, I'm clean."

Remeau forced himself to hold the gaze from the other man.

The Mexican said, "It cost a lot of money to get you and the strikers who went to jail with you off without charges. The lawyer who got you off was very influential, but it was a worthwhile expense. It saved Beacho a lot of money although they are moving the plant to Texas.

"My client told me to keep in touch with you. He said you never know when you might need someone who isn't overly concerned about hurting other people. We watched you attack those men as if you didn't care whether they lived or died."

Remeau shrugged and swallowed some of his drink. *What was he getting at?"*

"So that's why we're here. I want you to use your strength again. To injure someone, just one man. I need him hurt so badly he will need to be hospitalized indefinitely?"

The Mexican was staring into his face.

Holys shit. The man had him figured as some kind of hit man. Sure. he was right about how he whacked at those old guys, but he didn't do it for fun. He was paid and the Mexican had better have more than five thousand in mind for this job.

Ordonez leaned across the table. "It's a coincidence you found the best possible location for the target. Yes, you must injure the man you've been watching, the pitcher, Clay Burnside. He has to be hurt so bad that he will spend the rest of the baseball season in a hospital bed. Could you do that for twenty five thousand dollars?"

51

Naomi was busy, most of it now routine , preparing ads for Preston's planned tour through the southern tier of Louisiana, Mississippi, Alabama, and Florida. She and her two aides were still handling calls, mostly from readers of Clay's ads, but not in the volume that poured in the first days after they ran.

The response Preston approved was very close to Naomi's first idea. She said the ads were filled with half-truths and exaggeration, and that his attacks were libelous. She had talked with a Beachco lawyer whose opinion was that the ads were not libelous, but there was no harm in telling callers that it was her opinion. She, Betty, and Amanda took the phone numbers and addresses of the callers, the idea being to send follow-up notes encouraging OSON interviews.

She saw Brian in the office several times a week, but all they could manage as a date was a couple of lunches. He was busy from morning until sometimes late at night, "getting it done."

"Press wants me to concentrate on people with job skills, men or women who can install electricity in houses and commercial build-ings, also in the new plants he hopes to have waiting for workers. We are going to need master plumbers and air conditioning specialists, home builders, people who can use a transit for laying out roadways and home sites. These people are usually doing okay right now, but Press will pay much more than they're getting now. I can't tell prospects how much more. I hope to get into that when he returns from this trip.

"He said we'll train the specialists we can't recruit here in the states. There's nothing the man and his brain trust hasn't thought out."

When she told him of her efforts to get phone numbers and addresses from interested callers, he said, "That's great. Try to learn how they make their livings, too."

He looked tired at their most recent meeting when lunch was brought into the office. She wondered if he wasn't finding the recruitment job more than he had bargained for. Or cared for.

She and her aides had several calls a day from the men, and women recruiters in other major cities. Preston or Jeremiah called in daily and she told them the reports were almost always upbeat. She said some of the recruiters said the Burnside ads were "awful, but didn't hurt their efforts."

She remembered Preston's remark that the ads would do less harm as time passed. She won-dered how harmful the ads would have become if Clay had stayed alive and continued his attacks. And added his voice. From her job with Canfield she knew his original signing bonus with the Giants and his current income and bonus plan. He was very wealthy and could have continued the attacks indefinitely.

Was that why he was killed? Could Preston have had anything to do with it? Ridiculous. But who else wanted him dead? They almost tore his arm off, and Sergeant Carey intimated the beastly act might be related to gambling interests, but she was sure he didn't think Clay was involved in fixing games.

Betty called her attention to some filing matters and Naomi tried to shove the mystery of his murder out of her mind. The tragedy would not be put away for long, even during sleeping hours. She awoke in the middle of the nights, wringing wet, shouting "Who? Why?"

52

Remeau and his partner found getting into the famous hotel unnoticed so easy they later laughed about it. They slipped through a crowd kitchen jammed with cooks and their aides shouting orders in a code at each other and the waiters shouting orders in a code of their own. It was Clements idea to go in through the kitchen and had checked out the back entrance the evening before their attack. A kitchen door opened onto an alley. They watched as kitchen people and dining room servers slipped out for smokes, not bothering to lock the door.

They guessed the brunette would show up around seven. They had no idea how long she would stay, but if her intent was to stay very long, maybe "for seconds," she would have to be left unconscious with her lover.

Remeau said. "She's a sweet looking lady. If there's time I might help myself to a piece."

Clements came up with stocking caps into which they cut eye holes. but if there was any danger of being recognized Burnside and the woman would have to die. Remeau didn't have a gun, but he had carried a switch blade since his teens.

The deal called for an advance payment of $10,000 in hundred dollar bills, delivered hand to hand in a Walgreen drug store. Remeau didn't haggle. He was impressed with the total for a job that didn't seem all that difficult. He would knock on the hotel door and when Burnside opened it he would hit him as many times as it took.

He would have taken less so obviously it was a big deal. He didn't need Clements to take out the pitcher, but had to admit he was helpful. He came up with the idea of going through the kitchen. He would give him five thou.

The deal was for the Mexican to pay the rest when it became public that the ballplayer was beaten up so badly he wouldn't be able to pitch again that season.

Clements said, "We should get out of my apartment as soon as you pick up the final payment. There's no reason to trust a guy who won't give you a name, even a phony one."

The kitchen was in major turmoil with servers yelling their orders and cooks and helpers scrambling to fill them. They moved quickly and unchallenged through the room and into a hallway where they found a freight elevator. They would have used the back stairs, but Clements said the stairwell doors would probably be locked.

On the fourth floor they decided to wait on the landing, They waited several minutes, then Clements took a peek down the hall, ducking back quickly.

He said, "I just saw a blonde get into the elevator."

Blonde? What the hell! The woman who left the envelope was brunette. Whatever, they had to get into 429.

They moved into the hallway and down it to 429. Another break, no one in the hallway. They needed another break for getting into the room without much noise. They had gone over several ideas for getting Burnside to open the door. Clements had the best plan.

"Give the door a couple of hard raps, and say, 'Hotel security,' then if he doesn't open up, say, not too loud, 'Mr. Burnside. we must speak with you.'"

The first idea worked, but the door barely inched open.

It was all they needed. Both men hit it hard, and Clay Burnside was knocked off his feet.

Then, the horror visualized by everyone who knew and loved the young man, from George and Myra Burnside, to the White Sox players and team officials, to Leo Carey, was realized.

There was no plan for the attack. Remeau said, "We'll just beat the shit out of him." It began when Clements yanked Burnside to his feet and had his forearm under the victim's chin and against his throat. Remeau, who had kicked the door shut, began the assault with unstoppable blows to the face. He heard bones snap, and he knew his victim was barely conscious. The young man made no effort to resist from the first crushing blow. His hands that had instinctively moved to fight off the attack now dangled at his side.

Neither man was an experienced mugger. Clements had never held anyone in the so-called "choke hold," no longer allowed in most law enforcement. He tightened his grip to keep the suddenly inert boy erect so that Remeau could continue his pounding.

Seeing his target helpless and unresponsive, Remeau remembered he was to injure the pitcher so badly he would not be able to pitch again for the rest of the year. He switched his attention to the pitcher's left arm.

Burnside might as well have been under sedation because he suffered no more torture. He was dead. The vicious wrenching Remeau applied to ruin one of baseball's best arms was as unnecessary as it was savage.

When he and Remeau slipped back through the luxury hotel's kitchen as easily as they came in Dick Clements was satisfied his role in the Burnside beating had earned him a share of Remeau's fee. When he saw the televised report of the murder the next morning, he spilled hot coffee all over his lap.

Born into a marriage of teen-agers a social worker called "dysfunctional," he was dumped into Chicago's parentless child system. His teachers agreed he was a bright kid, but lacking effort to do well. As with Remeau he was released into an economy of low-level jobs he hated. Easily led, he hooked up with a gang specializing in house break ins.

Learning the police had picked up one the gang, he guessed correctly that he would soon be named as a gang member. He used most of the cash in his wallet for a bus to Columbus, Ohio where a distant relative took him in and gave him a job in his paint store.

There was a girl, and when she told him she was pregnant, he ran, first eastward and jobs that barely produce living expenses, then back to Chicago after a jail sentence for attempted robbery.

Remeau's offer of rent money was welcome, but the news he was complicit in a murder left him numb and horrified, *Did Illinois execute murderers?*

He had to get out of Chicago, Far out, but he needed more than Remeau's five thousand. Jesus. He had to convince Remeau to go with him, part of the way, at least. If he took off alone and Remeau was picked up, he would surely blame him for killing the ballplayer.

He told Remeau, "We have to get out of town," but the big guy was iffy on the need to run."

He said. "Why? We can stand pat. We have plenty of cash to hole up. Besides, we have to wait for the Mex's call. I'm not running without the rest of the payoff."

Clements couldn't give up his doubts about staying in the city.

"Your Mex could rat us out and stiff us on the rest of the money. You don't how to find him, or even his name. All you have is a cell number and he could change that in a second."

Remeau hated the reminder of his loose connection with the Mexican, but his accomplice was right. Clements was smart. It was his idea to get into the hotel through the kitchen. He had the best idea for getting Burnside to open his door, too. He had fucked up by choking the ballplayer to death, but that was a mistake.

There was no call from the Mex and the murder pair spent the day and night watching anything on television other than murder news. Clements made them something to eat from leftovers in the fridge. Several times during the long hours he said, "Why did I hold that kid so long?"

When he hear the plaint, an annoyed Remeau snapped. "Forget it. It's over."

Remeau's cell buzzed an hour after their coffee and toast breakfast the next morning. He only listened, saying, "I got it," to end the forty-second call. He grinned at Clements.

"The Mex is leaving the money in a toilet in Jackson park. He said I can pick it up in an hour. The park's an easy walk from here so I won't take the car. You use it to get us food for a couple of weeks, at least."

They finished their breakfast which was tasteless for Clements, but Remeau's lack of concern somehow helped ease his horror for what he had done.

As he left Remeau said, I'll call you if there is any problems. "

Clements knew what he would do, whether Remeau called or not. He would get them ready to run. He didn't dare use the car for groceries. The cops would have a dragnet, picking up anyone looking suspicious. They would talk to the Palmer House kitchen crew. Those people were busy and seemed to pay no attention to them as they slipped in and out, but someone might have noticed them.

He slammed shirts, sox and underwear into a suitcase, and filled another with   belongings. He also packed Remeau's small suitcase. The big man traveled light. At the apartment door he looked down the street both ways before throwing the luggage into Remeau's Ford trunk. He looked up and down the street again before getting behind the wheel.

He couldn't take off on his own. How far could be get on the five thousand? If Remeau called to say he had been stiffed, he would pick him up as he left the park. If the Mex hadn't left the cash it would be very likely the son of a bitch dropped a dime on them.

What made Remeau so sure he could trust the man? He could see Remeau sweating as the cops pounded him with questions.

Remeau's judgment that the Mexican would pay him off had to be right. The man could easily be on his back in Kansas, or wherever, with the fifteen thou. He patted the wheel. The money had to be there, but why such a weird drop off place? Jesus, another thing to worry about. Would Remeau take off with the rest of the pay off?

Relax. The big guy would need a car. He wasn't smart enough to work out a scheme for taking off without wheels.

It had been more than forty minutes. How far did the man have to go in the park?

Finally. He gave the steering wheel a slap of relief. He saw Remeau in the mirror, trotting up the sidewalk, carrying a paper bag. He jumped out of the car and led his breathless, soaking wet partner into the apartment.

"What happened?"

"I think I fucked the Mex. What the hell were you doing in the car?"

Clements told him. Remeau nodded.

"That was smart, but I would've called if the cash wasn't there."

Remeau shucked off his clothes in the kitchen.

"I thought he might be waiting for me near that toilet. There was no one near the place to witness anything . I figured he might try to hijack our money, maybe leave me for dead, so I took no chances."

"Get this. I found the toilet, no problem, but I wasn't going in the front door. I waded through a lagoon behind the shit hole, and squeezed through an open back window. I was kind of surprised he played it square. The package was where he said he'd leave it.

"I took no chance he might be waiting for me. I went out the window and back through the lagoon. I was leaving the park when I heard a bunch of Black assholes yakking it up about a meeting they're going to. One of them yelled at me. He said 'Hey White boy. You want us back in Africa. This guy is going to give us our own country."

"I stopped and got the dope. The meeting is tonight in a hotel a mile from here. It might be something to do."

Remeau had picked up a Sun-Times from a street-side box on his way back to the apartment. Clements ignored the headlines that screamed the murder and was flipping pages when he saw the banner headline for Burnside's ad. He read the words of the man he had helped kill. Shaking and speechless he held out the paper to Remeau who was putting his clothes back in a drawer.

Remeau had hardly begun to scan the attack when he muttered, "Holy shit. Yeah, we gotta hear this guy. It looks like Burnside wanted to wreck a good idea?"

The meeting held in the hotel's banquet room was packed with standing room only. The full-page Burnside attack on OSON had attracted almost as many Whites as Blacks. They found chairs in the back of the room, sitting several feet apart.

Beach began his speech with his shock and regrets for Burnside's murder, then did his usual thirty minutes on OSON and its goals before opening the session for questions. The first question from a young Black man was whether the Burnside attack would harm the OSON movement.

Beach was prepared for the question as he was at the meeting the night before.

"I cannot say the young man's attack coupled with his murder is a hiccup for OSON. His passion for his views is undeniable and well stated, and he has made his appeal nationwide, but we are also laying our plan before the entire nation, and the world. We offer opportunity now. The Burnside position offers uncertain hope for future generations."

When the meeting broke they were moving toward the door when Remeau grabbed Clements's arm. He jerked his head toward two men huddled at the edge of the crowd.

"Jesus, It's my Mex. The little fucker hired me for that job in Kansas City, and the tall nigger must have been in on it, too. I saw them together outside the Kansas City jail."

Clements grabbed an OSON pamphlet at the door. In the car back to the apartment, Remeau said, "There's gotta be some sort of connection here. It's a cinch this OSON outfit hated Burnside.

What the hell. We wiped out the big shot's enemy for peanuts. That job was worth a lot more."

Clements said, "Hell yes. Give me a couple of minutes to think this out."

Clements sat at the kitchen table with the OSON pamphlet. Its Chicago headquarters was listed on the first page with the names Jeremiah Constable, Executive Vice President, Naomi Stafford, Vice President of Communications. Both were listed under that of OSON's founder and president Preston Beach.

Clements said. "Call the Mex. Tell him you are on the way out of the country, but you need a lot more cash to stay out of the states. That will be forever, tell him."

Reneau shook his head. "He won't believe that. He'll set me up somehow to get killed. I think he was going to kill me in the park."

"Not if we tell him you have a letter that will go to the cops if you are harmed in any way. You can read it to him over the phone. It will say that he is the man who hired you to injure Burnside.

"Sign it, an eye witness."

As soon as the words were out of his mouth Clements grabbed his head with both hands

"Shit, what's with my mind. Even if the Mex takes your call you don't have his name. Chicago has a zillion Mexicans.

"I'm trying to put this together too fast. We can't prove the men we saw at the meeting are the same two in Kansas City?"

"Yeah. So?"

"If the Black guy you saw with the Mex in Kansas City is Beach's man he could be more important than someone who sets up a strike break. What's he doing in Chicago?"

Clements held up the OSON plugger.

"He could even be this guy, Constable."

"How can we be sure?"

Clements wasn't going to insult his partner by inferring the big man was a dummy.

He said, "The KC chamber of commerce will have that dope. And remember. You got off free down there. No charges. Someone put in the fix. We've got a chance for some real money, pal. We just have to figure a way to connect these people with the order to shut up the pitcher. Beach could be behind it all. If the man you saw at the meeting is Constable, we can ask for a lot of money, why not a million? Give him three, or maybe four days. We can get passports that soon and we have to come up with a foolproof idea for the drop off. And we have to get out of Chicago."

Remeau liked Clements's quick take on things, but he was still doubtful. "Let's sleep on it. Make sure of the ident of the guy with the Mex."

"Okay, but we shouldn't sleep here. Your Mexican may know where we're holed up. If you got away with the cash he planned to hijack, he will be pissed. What if he pulls a cross by turning you in with an anonymous phone call.

Remeau picked up his suitcase.

"Okay. Let's get something to eat and find a new hideout."

"No problem. All I have in here is clothes and some stuff we might need."

54

They found a hot-bed five-story hotel on Grand Crossing avenue. Clements tapped a bell to rouse a shoelace-thin seventy-year old male who stared at the pair through a steel mesh screen. He was estimating their chances of staying the whole night

"Sixty two fifty. We don't take credit cards."

In the room Clements said, "We're lucky they have a room with two beds. The old man thinks we're queer. That's okay. It couldn't be a better place to disappear. Let's get some sleep."

Remeau was in deep slumber in seconds, but it was a long night for Clements. He thrashed on the aged mattress. Jesus, the blood, and the poor kid's smashed in face.

They picked up breakfast at a McDonald's drive through. Back in their room Clements had a new idea.

He said, "I brought some paper from the apartment. Here, take my pen and work on a letter while I make the call."

Clements had once thought he would use up the minutes on the cell he grabbed from Clay Burnside's sports coat, but saw the theft as a bad idea before they were out of the hotel. The stolen cell went into a street side waste container. Both he and Remeau now had cheap cells. He sat on the edge of a bed and had no trouble getting through to the Kansas City chamber of commerce.

He was switched to an obliging young female who he told he was with the Los Angeles Times and that he needed information for an article he was doing on the Beachco corporation.

He had a willing helper. She first confirmed that the struck plant was owned by Beachco.

"They're leaving town, you know. Lots of bad will in the community."

Clements said, "I'm sorry to hear that."

He led his informant into the structure of Beachco management. A few moments later he learned that Jeremiah Constable held a post as VP and executive assistant to Mr. Beach.

"He's a colored man, you know."

Clements grinned at Remeau. Gave him a thumbs up.

The woman asked, did he need anything more? The corporation's annual report?

"No thank you, but I appreciate your generous help. Have a nice day in Kansas City."

He held up the vee sign. "What a break. How could I have asked if Constable was Black? He's got to be the man we saw with the Mex last night.

"Forget about trying to get in touch with the Mex. For all we know the Burnside thing could have come from the top, Beach, but let's mail our letter to Constable. We know his connection with your Mexican. It'll shake him up. I'll tell him I'll call him in three days. That'll give us time for our passports. I know where to get them in a hurry."

Clements was a better than average scholar before being released into society. He remembered Jimmy Remeau, a fun-loving but disruptive classmate in grade school. He saw no harm in letting the man move in with him, and they may have teamed up for some productive jobs, but that's not going to happen now. He was a wanted man and getting out of the country with Beachco cash was the only option. He was going to have to ditch Remeau, but he would worry about that later.

Remeau had made a stab at the Constable letter. Clements said, "Pretty good, but let me have a shot at it."

Clements worked carefully, tearing up two tries. He signed the approved version per his original idea, "A witness." He added "Private and Personal" on the envelope. He then wrote a copy of the short letter for the cops. He addressed the envelope to the Chicago Police Department, folded it once and stuffed it in a jacket pocket.

Both men agreed a beer would taste good. They adjourned to the Bear.

Clements said, "We can order messenger service from there."

55

Leo thought it was time to interview Preston Beach. He called OSON, identified himself, and asked for Naomi Stafford .

"Hey, Sergeant Carey. How are you doing?"

"Fine. I'm interested in talking with Mr. Beach. Can you arrange a meeting for me."

"Of course, May I tell him what it's all about?"

"Sure, and you don't have to make a guess. It will be about the Clay Burnside murder."

She wasn't surprised. She had wondered why he hadn't called before.

"Mr. Beach just wound up a trip. He may be resting in his hotel, the Ambassador. Let me try and I'll get back to you within a few minutes. Okay?"

"Okay. How're doing over there?"

"Busy, but we're getting by. I don't suppose you'd tell me if you had anything new?"

"Probably not, but I'd be tempted."

She laughed. "All right, Sergeant. I'll be right back."

And she was. "He said he would welcome your call. Call him on his cell." She gave him the number.

He wrote the number on his pad, then punched it out. Beach picked up on the first ring.

Leo didn't have to identify himself.

"Sergeant Carey, how are you. Naomi tells me you are twenty four seven on the Burnside case. What a tragedy for Chicago and the game of baseball."

"Yes it is, Mr. Beach, and I'd like to do a one –on- one with you in connection with the case. You must be aware that the ads placed by Clay Burnside since his death make your OSON movement a possible suspect."

"Yes, it's ridiculous, but understandable.

Where would you like to meet? Should I have an attorney with me?"

"I'll come there. Use your judgment about a lawyer."

They made the date for late in the afternoon, in Beach's suite. Leo thought he'd ask Henry to come with him if he was available. He was.

Henry kidded, "Do you think he will try to ply us with drink, "

"Why not? We're off the clock, aren't we?"

A door man pointed toward a ramp at the end of the building. It led up to parking. From there they found a bank of elevators that took them took them to the top of the building.

A tall, African-American opened the suite door and introduced himself as Jeremiah Constable. Leo remembered seeing him at the meeting he attended with Sid. Beach stood as they entered the living room. With him was the attractive woman Leo remembered as having introduced Beach at the meeting. She smiled and held out her hand.

"I'm Pamela Kirsten, an aide to Mr. Beach."

She didn't add that she had a law degree from the University of Chicago, and had been admitted to the bar. It had earned her the job with OSON.

Everyone shook hands.

Beach said, "I'm sure it's been a long day, Sergeants. Will you have something to drink?

Leo said, "I'd enjoy a beer." Henry nodded his approval for the same. There were several varieties available. They settled on Michaelob.

They were settled in chairs with their drinks. Constable and Kirsten shared a couch. Leo got things going.

"We're satisfied two men were involved, but they may not have wanted Burnside dead. We thought that because they went to the special trouble of almost tearing the boy's arm out of its socket. They may have done this to help some gambling interests, or they wanted us to think that was the case.

"But then the Burnside ads ran, beginning immediately after he was killed. If you had wanted to prevent the attack, it was too late, but there's still the possibility you or someone wanted to punish him for attacking the OSON movement."

Beach's face had lost its tan when Leo described the murder. Several seconds passed before he spoke. He leaned forward holding his drink.

"I have to agree, Sergeant, but as I said when we talked this morning, the idea is ridiculous. First, had we known the ads were going to run we would have appealed to Mr. Burnside to sit down with us and try to reach a compromise. Looking back, I believe we could have worked something out. He spoke a lot of truth, but he didn't have all the facts. And he was making a judgment on the thinking of Black Americans. OSON is making that judgment, too, but our thinking is based on face-to-face meetings with thousands of people over the past several years."

Leo didn't want to hear Beach's pitch all over again. The man was on a roll. He had stated the case for OSON all over the nation. He had it all down pat. Leo had to interrupt if he was to get anything worth the trouble of calling the meeting.

He held up a hand.

"The trouble we see is that Burnside's argument may have been so strong to someone that they felt he had to be stopped. He was a wealthy young man, obviously passionate about his feelings. He could have continued his OSON attack indefinitely.

"He was killed before the first one hit. Maybe there was a leak, and the people behind the killing couldn't get their murderous scheme together in time to shut him up."

It was a long speech. Leo sucked in a lung full of air.

Beach said. "I've talked with some of the all-White America loonies. They are solidly in our camp, their support wanted or not. They could have killed the boy, but the mutilation of the arm seems to point to a gambling connection."

Leo said, "We are checking out that angle. but a priority right now is finding a man we think led the assault. He is James Reneau, He was raised in Chicago by a family of that name, but was in trouble and left the city in his late teens. He lived in California for several years, and spent some time in jail out there. We believe he is in Chicago. Have you ever heard of this man?"

"No."

The meeting lapsed into small talk. Beach said he had commiserated over Burnside's death with White Sox owner Walt Konenberger.

"He is a solid supporter of OSON, Sergeant."

In their car, Leo said, "Beach's remark about Konenberger did little for my mood. Jesus, are we going to have to interview him, too?"

Jeremiah Constable was in shock. A messenger might just well have handed him a stick of ignited dynamite. He gave the brief poisonous message only a few seconds before twisting it into shreds.

It must have been authored by Remeau's fellow thug. Ordonez had told him Remeau was an ignorant lout.

They wanted to get out of the country. He very much wanted them out of the country. He could pay them. He had unquestioned access to OSON funds, but that wouldn't end it. They would come back, want more. The right solution would be to see them dead.

Ordonez was on their trail. He did well in maintaining contact with Remeau, and the brute's surveillance over Burnside had uncovered the perfect place for the attack. It was to look gambler-involved, but the total whitewash of the young man made that assumption ridiculous. The cop, Carey, made that clear. Somehow the police had tracked Remeau and identified him as the Burnside killer. The goon he had seen break the auto parts strike went savage in that hotel room.

The publicist, Carrington, had warned him that Burnside was likely to initiate some kind of anti-OSON campaign, but the speed with which he put together the nation-wide full-page thing was a shock and amazing.

Ordonez had to beat the police in finding Remeau. He had called with a questionable report on missing Remeau in Jackson park where he said he had placed the second part of Remeau's fee.

He said, "The son of a bitch got the money and got away. Somehow I missed him."

It sounded like an alibi. He probably kept the money for himself, but if he wanted see more money he still had to be find and eliminate Remeau. Along with his literate partner. The note said he had three days to come up with the money before a copy of his note went to the police. He had to stall the insane creatures until Ordonez found them.

What a tragic screw up. The plan he had put before Preston five years ago was threatened by a baseball player. It was making him ill. All the years of poverty, the struggle for an education, the years in Africa. the decision not to marry,

During the search for meaningful work after the African years he learned Beachco of Kansas City had a liberal policy about minorities. The huge company had Black majorities in several of its unions. Constable was hired by Beachco industrial relations to help negotiate contracts. He poured in the hours, was recognized for his community relations skills in plant communities, and ultimately became the "token negro" executive in the Beachco empire.

As department Vice President he was credited with maintaining harmony with three hundred thousand employees and dozens of unions. His first mistake was the Kansas City auto parts mess. Two workers nearly killed, and the huge cost of moving the plant.

Beach forgave him.

He said, You were doing your best to save us a lot of money."

He was promoted to VP several years before. Beach had invited him into his office.

"No one has worked harder for a position of leadership, Constable. I consider myself a liberal person, but your promotion has nothing to do with the color of your skin."

Beach encouraged him to talk about himself.

It was a typical story. He described another Black kid with no ambition beyond perfecting a hook shot.

"My father cleared out early. My mother was more ambitious for me than I was. She actually walked with me to school, afraid I would ditch classes, but I got interested and scholarships and government-supported education did the rest."

Conversations with the top executive were more frequent after he had his own corner office. The awareness the big boss was liberal led to the day he describing his dream of a new African state.

He remembered his surprise and pleasure when Beach heard him out with the original idea for what became OSON. The man not only listened patiently, but inserted good questions. When he heard him describe how the excellent sites for the new nation could be procured, he leaned back and laughed.

"Jeremiah, this is no silly dream. Let's make a hole in my schedule so we can really get into your idea."

Later Beach, who came up with the name, OSON said, "Suppose we pull it off? We

take the cream and leave the junkies and convicts and government supported families and their progeny behind. What happens then?"

He answered, "If we succeed the U.S. government will have to do more to help Blacks fill the void created by OSON. America will be better because of a successful OSON."

Beach believed that.

"You are right, Jeremiah. Our success will help America."

57

Leo took a call from a newsman he barely knew. Buck Baron of the Sun-Times. Baron wrote sports after gaining local fame as Babe Baronowski, a hard hitting line backer for a championship north-side prep team. Over the years he moved into special features and then as Sid Coffin's counterpart at the tabloid.

Leo met him at the press club. Baron said then. "Sidney, I should have a cop buddy like Sergeant Carey."

He said, "I'm checking an anonymous tip. I've learned that Mrs. Matt Holiday is the second blonde you've been looking for. She was in room 429."

Leo had surprises over his career, but this shocker hit him like an armor-piercing bullet. Who told him?

It couldn't be Henry? Who else was possible? Only Phelan and Bradshaw. He would stake his career that it wasn't Phelan. Anything confidential he told his mentor and friend went into a mental lock box.

That meant Bradshaw!

He was stunned into silence. Baron said, "Leo, are you there?"

"Yeah, You want me to confirm a rumor?"

"Leo, let's not play games. My source is impeccable. What I would like to know is whether Coffin got the same tip and what he plans to do with it."

Your source was impeccable, all right. . The son of a bitch is a Lieutenant in one of the largest, best run police organizations in the world. Of course he would be believed.

Sid said he would sit on it to help save a marriage, but rat Bradshaw didn't suggest Baron hold the explosive item for the same merciful idea?

Leo said, "If I had the news of Mrs. Holiday's infidelity and relayed it to the man with whom I've had a tight friendship for many years, I would expect him to sit on it based on our friendship with Matt Holiday and our mutual feeling that Chicago doesn't need another shock to go with the murder of a fine young man."

"Hey, that's a helluva speech, Leo. Mine will be much shorter. I will sit on the item, too. What about the DA?"

"They only know that I'm convinced Sissy Holiday had nothing to do with Clay Burnside's murder."

"Okay, thanks, Leo."

"Oh, thank you, Buck."

58

Constable picked up the call on his cell.

Ordonez. "I'm in my car outside a restaurant called the Bear. The two people we are interested in are having drinks at the bar. Should I meet with them as we discussed?"

Constable paused. Was this too easy? How in hell had Ordonez found these two bumblers so soon?

He said, "Are you sure?"

"Absolutely. I'll be pleased to report on how I plan to conduct the meeting."

This was cloak and dagger talk Ordonez thought necessary, but it was easily understood.

Constable said, "Please go ahead with the assignment."

He didn't like the Mexican, but he had delivered good news. Marvelous. How good it would be to hear his report. And to read and hear the media coverage that followed. As usual, he erased the message.

It was difficult to return to OSON tasks. He had a meeting upcoming with young Brian Strang. in the morning. The young lawyer was doing a terrific job, but needed help. He called Naomi at her apartment.

"Brian needs help. Can you give him some names from your local contacts?"

She said, "I know we have several. I'll give them to you tomorrow morning."

He thought what a treasure she had become.

Burnside's murder had shaken her badly, but she was coming out of it. Wouldn't it be terrible if she learned he was involved. It would be terrible period. It would wreck the movement. Now, the news Burnside's killers were dead might be some compensation for her loss. He could hardly wait for Ordonez's follow up report.

Chaos in the Bear. Two men had just been shot. Both victims went down and the gunman had fled. One victim lay still. The other, blood running from wounds, struggled to his feet and staggered after the shooter.

Sal Baiano called Leo's office number, but. Leo and off-duty Henry were already driving to the restaurant for a late snack. Driver Henry jammed his foot on the accelerator before they heard the complete relayed message. Leo called for back up. They pulled up, roof lights blazing, guns drawn. Baiano was on the sidewalk with several gawking civilians.

He ran to Leo.

"You just missed him. I think he was Mexican, a little guy. He came in and yelled, 'Hey, big guy' at the two men at the bar.

"The man he called out knew the man. He said, 'What the fuck are you doing here?' and the Mexican shot him.

"The other man ran for the door and the Mexican shot him. Then the first man, the big guy, tried to get up and tackle the Mexican and the Mexican shot him again, He yelled, 'Now you are not so strong, big guy,' and he ran out the door.

"The big man got up and ran after him. The floors all bloody." He repeated, "You just missed him."

Henry reached for Baiano's arm, to calm the man. Leo went into the Bear. He called over his shoulder, "Make the calls."

Some back-up uniforms pulled up. Henry ordered them to tape the area and look for witnesses. He then called for a crime investigation team

The restaurant was not crowded. One booth held a pair of late-night office workers. Another was filled with three telephone company repair men An alarmed Corrine had an arm around Leo's waist. He would remember this touch of intimacy. The arm slipped away as he bent over the young man sprawled on his stomach a few feet from the door. He hoped he was only wounded. Not so. A single bullet had caught the young man in the back of his head.

He pulled gloves from a pocket and went on his knees beside the dead man. He risked being scolded by the investigators, but he didn't need to move the victim to find and pull free a stuffed wallet.

"Hey." He held up a handful of one hundred dollar bills.

He called out, "Louis," but the cook was already standing behind him.

"Know this guy?"

"Nope, never saw him, or the other guy."

Leo spoke to the quiet room. "Please take a look people. Anyone seen this man or the other man before? Anyone hear any names?"

The answers from the booths was a chorus of nos.

Sal said, "They've been in several times the past several days."

Sal's bartender, Fred Haney, who had gone down behind the bar after the first shot, agreed. "Yeah, they only drank beer. They talked but I heard nothing."

Corrine said, "I served them but they didn't say anything to me and I didn't hear anything."

Leo looked up at Henry who had news.

"Sal said the shooter was wearing black slacks and a bright red shirt. One of our back-up guys collared a witness who said the first man running from the Bear drove off in a tan Chevrolet Malibu. He said the wounded man drove an old Ford. He wasn't sure of the color, thought it might be blue."

Leo had added a driver's license to his findings in the dead man's wallet.

He said, "Bob, this guy is Richard Clements, loaded with new one hundred dollar bills. Where did this cash come from? It could be pay-off money. It's crazy, but we need to get a head shot of Remeau in front of these people."

Henry grinned, "No problem." He reached into a pocket. "I've been lugging a shot of this guy since Carole gave it to me."

A minute later everyone in the room confirmed the big man was James Remeau. The all-points search now had a wounded man's name along with his description.

60

Leo had never had a call like the one just ended. He smashed a fist on his desk. He believed Baron was going to keep his word, but it was still a stunner to learn the reporter had a man inside the Chicago police department.

Bradshaw was among three other people who knew of Sissy's confession. Henry? Of course not. Phelan? Anything confidential he had ever told his boss-mentor was locked in a mental safe.

Bradshaw! Good God. His instinct was to run into the prick's office, grab him around the throat, and choke him unconscious.

No way, but he had to come up with punishment to match the incredible act.

Leo's friendship with the Tribune's Sid Coffin was known by the general public as well as by the department. He had solved two major crimes with Sid's help along with numerous citations over his more than twenty years of service. He would have been given the post held by Bradshaw, but for his choice to continue a more active role in the street. Leo rarely gave Coffin anything he didn't release to the media in general. If he gave Sid an advance tip it usually was with the condition it be held until it could be released generally.

Why would Bradshaw do this? Tipping the Sissy Holiday confession was pure treachery.

His concentration on how he would injure Bradshaw eclipsed his normal day, even the Burnside case. There was a way. He slept on his decision. Should he tell Phelan? No, not for this.

He called Bradshaw the next morning, asking if he could come to his office.

"Sure, what's up?"

Leo had rarely visited Bradshaw alone. When he saw him, it was with Phelan in Phelan's office. He didn't dislike the man, at least until now, but he sent him the usual paper, keeping him in touch with his activity. He thought that was all that was necessary.

Bradshaw looked up. The visit was unusual. He tried not to dislike Carey, but Carey had kept too much distance and it was irksome. Why had he come in now?

He asked again, "What's up?"

Leo said, "I'm going to address the troops and I want you to listen in."

Leo knew his decision to punish Bradshaw was harsh. But he was certain it was deserved. What he was about to do could backfire, but he would risk the stain on his own reputation.

Bradshaw frowned. "Can't you tell me first?"

"I could, but then I would have to repeat myself, and it would be a waste of time."

Bradshaw pulled himself out of his chair.

"Okay."

The large squad room was filled with men and women, ready to go to their cars or to pursue other assignments. Leo held up a hand and called out. "May I have your attention, please."

He got all ears within seconds. There wasn't an officer in the room who didn't know Leo's career adventures that made national headlines. He was the cop who early in his career had jumped onto a speeding truck and saved a girl's life. His career was like something out of the movies

Leo had rehearsed his speech, and it came out fast and hard.

"We all are on the lookout for James Remeau, who we think is the Clay Burnside killer. Good luck, but be careful. Remeau may not be armed, but handle any contact as if he would kill to make his getaway.

"I have a story in connection with the case I think you should hear.

"Two days ago Bob Henry and I learned something important to the solution of the case. We decided against releasing the news and its source to the media. It was our judgment the item, while sensational, would have sent a shock throughout Chicago that would have made the Burnside murder even more painful."

"Yesterday, I had a call from Buck Baron of the Sun-Times who said he had an anonymous call that described the shocking news. He knows my long association with Sid Coffin of the Trib and wanted to know if I was going to release the item to my friend. I told him no. I was a very happy cop when he said he would take the same position."

Leo saw Commander Jim Phelan standing in his office doorway across the room. He had heard all he wanted to hear or all he wanted his staff to hear. He shouted, "Leo," and made an urgent wave for him to come into his office. The captain, for a reason he would soon give, had sensed what his long-time favorite was up to.

Bradshaw, though not invited, was already walking fast to join Phelan. His face was brick red.

Leo said to a roomful of upturned faces, "That's all I have right now, people. As you were."

Phelan was not outwardly angry, but he was standing behind his desk, not a good sign. Bradshaw was standing, too, obviously furious, holding a handkerchief against his sweating face.

Phelan stared at his friend and favorite cop.

"Leo, were you so angry that you decided to wreck a career?"

Leo had sold himself that Bradshaw would be hurt badly, but would survive his charge. Now, in the face of Phelan's question. he had to admit Bradshaw would have lost all respect from his fellow cops.

"I thought it out. I wanted to hurt this guy, and I couldn't think of a more painful way.

"Bradshaw, you wouldn't have put on the gloves with me in the gym. I would have knocked the piss out of you."

Phelan sat down, but he didn't point to chairs for the men he intended to discipline..

He said, "Bradshaw, snitching that story showed me a side to your character I don't like. I'm going to have you transferred."

Bradshaw, relieved that Phelan didn't come up with something worse, decided he would not try to excuse his action as no worse than Carey's communication with Sid Coffin.

Phelan said, "I'll spank you later, Leo. Now get out of here, both of you."

61

Remeau was back in the rundown hotel room. The wounds ached, but bleeding had eased up. He felt safe enough. The Mexican scumbag thought he was dead. What a fuck up. They never should never have been in that bar. The Mex had somehow tracked them down.

Where was the Mex now? Probably collecting his money for killing him and Clements, then on his way back to KC, or wherever. Trying to find him would be a waste of time, but he had to square things with his boss.

The blood had soaked up his shirt and oozed into his underwear. The slugs must have been small caliber. One slug had passed through the fleshy part of his shoulder, the other was still in his left side, had nicked a rib. It was good that he was stunned and went down. He had tried to get his hands on the little greaser. He would have torn him into small chunks, but it was just as well he stayed down. The scumbag might have put a couple more slugs in him.

It was too bad about Clements. He had a way for getting passports and he would have had ideas on where to go. The cops would get

Clements's five thousand. He had the cop copy of the Constable letter in his jacket, too. The wallet was sticking out of his back pocket. He should have grabbed it, and the letter, but the cop sirens were screaming.

He should get out of the city, but he had never wanted to get even more. He remembered how he had punished the little kids who snitched on him at the home. Kid stuff, but he was always had to get revenge. He had to kill Constable, maybe the Mex somehow.

Constable had to be scared like Clements said, but if the cops didn't come after him tonight there was no reason for him not to go to his office in the morning. Clements said the letter itself was not enough for an arrest. The man's lawyer would tell him he could only be a person of interest like in the movies. It's late, they'll wait until tomorrow if they come at all, but if they decide to come in the morning he had to kill the bastard quick and get the hell out of town.

He would park as close as possible to the office and sleep in the car. Right now he had to get cleaned up and find a gun. Every nigger in this part of Chicago had at least one. A few hundred bucks might buy him an arsenal.

Clements had brought a ton of stuff from his apartment besides clothes. He dug into a bag that had scissors and tape and kitchen stuff including a can opener. It was easy to rip one of the hotel's cheap towels into strips and bind both the shoulder and body wounds. He would get some disinfectant from an all-night drug store.

He wouldn't come back to the hotel. If the desk man decided to make points with the cops by describing him, he was wasting his time. And theirs.

He took the slow boat China elevator and had a flash of optimism when he saw a bald elderly Black man dozing behind the steel mesh.

He said, "Hey" and waved a pair of
hundreds. "I need a gun."

The late-night manager came alert very quickly. He peered at the large young man whose look described a person about to make a bad decision. He's seen the impatience, the tightness around the eyes, many times before.

He no longer offered stop-and-think counsel.

"Make it five more of them nice Cees and I'll sell you my own very reliable Colt revolver with a handful of shells."

Remeau grunted approval. If he'd had a smile left in him he would have used it. He'd been given a time-saving a break.

He was on his way downtown moments later. If he could kill Constable, he would be a happy man heading for wide open spaces.

62

Leo stood over medical examiner Gene Kosloski as he turned over the body. Gene's crew and Leo, Bob Henry, and Sal Baiano were the only persons left in the Bear.

Gene first checked the head wound. "Small caliber, probably thirty eight. Lucky shot for the shooter, not so lucky for the young man."

The small revolver was standard issue for Leo's granddad. It was seldom used except on the target range, but when the FBI came to town to duel the liquor mobs, and the city was scourged by alcohol and drug-created crime that followed, something with more "stopping power" was needed. Leo and most of his mates carried at least nine millimeter weapons. Some of them had a smaller gun strapped to an ankle.

Leo quoted Baiano,

"Sal said the big man was hit twice but he got off the floor and ran out of here. He's not likely to die, but he'll need bandages and disinfectant. We'll send uniforms to check out drug stores."

Clements was wearing a leather jacket. Kosloski poked through its pockets. He said, "What's this?"

Leo, still wearing his plastic gloves, carefully pulled the one-sheet message from the folded unsealed envelope addressed to the Chica-go Police department. He scanned Clement's brief, message, read it again, and pursed his lips for a whistle with no sound.

"Wow!" and read it again.

Back in a relatively quiet office Leo went into Carole's office where she had filed some special files he wanted saved. He found what he needed in a few seconds, pulled it free, and returned to his office to call Phelan. The Captain was watching a late night ball game, but he was instantly alert from his ace detective's news

"It sounds like a major break, Leo, but the witness claims seeing Constable in Kansas City, then at a Chicago OSON meeting, but the letter can't prove Constable ordered the Burnside attack. The writer said he saw Constable with a Mexican at both sites, but who is the Mexican? The letter doesn't even have a name."

Leo said, We may not be dead on the Mex. The Chevy might be a rental. Henry has a crew covering every agency in the city. The Mex had to show an ID. We could get lucky."

"We can hope so, but congratulations on finding the note. Let's discuss further strategy first thing in the morning."

"Okay, but I have an idea for getting a warrant and picking up Constable tonight.

"Remember the Hodiak case. Before our time. Wally Montgomery was a Lieutenant then and he took something even more circumstantial to Judge Dick Baldwin. He got a warrant, and finally a trial and a conviction, because Baldwin agreed the coincidences linked together too coincidentally."

"So?"

I'd like to go to call Baldwin tonight with another string of coincidences. It's not too late.

"I can tell him that we can trace Constable and his Mexican back to Kansas City and that some strikers will remember seeing Remeau with the Mexican. They would have seen the Mexican with Constable, too. We may get a name for the Mex. Someone may remember seeing a pay off.

"Transfer the scene to Chicago. Our note writer said he saw them together here and we can confirm that. Maybe they were seen together in the Ambassador coffee shop, or in neighboring restaurants.

We'll get on that when we get Constable's head shot. It should be here in a couple of hours. Baldwin should still be up and I can get to his condo in twenty minutes."

"Okay, give it a try after your warrant. Call me back either way."

63

Alex Ordonez was still in Chicago, parked in an alley a mile from the Ambassador hotel.. He found something to eat at a Taco restaurant drive through. Phony Mexican food, but tasty.

He thought the cops must be on a city-wide search for his rental. Someone at the restaurant must have seen him drive away. By the time they checked all the agencies, and learned he used a phony ID, he'd be long gone from this cow town.

He had to see Constable. The man hadn't paid him a dime yet and he had earned a helluva fee. Jesus, he had just eliminated the only people who could link him to the ballplayer's murder.

It was a pleasure putting Remeau down. He didn't like the man, maybe because of his size, or the way he held him up in Kansas City, but he was a punk. Just a big one. Whatever. The shot that killed his buddy was pure luck He had never. aimed the Beretta at a man. Fired it at tin cans. Now he was a mass murderer.

It was possible Remeau was alive. His automatic was a small model, only a thirty eight. He bought it because it was light and fit in a pocket.

If Remeau wasn't dead he was hurt bad.

He was too bad he missed him at the park. park. When he left the toilet he was going to walk up to him and say "Never disrespect a Mexican," shoot him in the face.

The big man almost got away, but he caught up with him. He hid behind some bushes and saw Remeau talking to some Black kids. He followed him to the apartment, but thought he would need his car and trotted back to the park. He drove to a spot across the street from the apartment with the idea of shooting Remeau in his room, but it would be hard to take him by surprise. He might have picked up a gun, too. He would wait, sleep in the car if necessary, but the man had to get something to eat.

He had something to think about. The cash from Constable .

Suddenly Remeau appeared with a male companion. They each carried suitcases.

Jesus, it has to be Remeau's buddy.

He had no trouble following Remeau's Ford to a crappy hotel. He was prepared to wait again, this time overnight, but they appeared again. He again followed, thinking they must be going for something to eat, and had another surprise. They drove to the hotel where Beach was holding another OSON meeting.

64

Henry called in. The worn out policeman wasn't happy, even with the huge overtime he was earning.

"It was a National agency at O'Hare. They confirmed the car and the Mexican renter, but we're having trouble connecting the driver's license and credit card with a believable owner."

"Okay, any leads on the big guy?"

"Nothing yet. There are a hell of a lot of drugstores. Maybe he won't look for disinfectant. I don't think he was hurt all that bad. The small slugs knocked him down, but he got up and ran after the shooter. He didn't stay down so we'll alert all hospital EMs."

"All right. At least we have a pretty sure thing on who killed Burnside."

"Okay, see in the morning."

"Wait a minute. We need a head shot of Constable. Put Carole to work on it. He was a top Beachco executive. They should have all kinds of pix of the man. Get the KC cops in on it."

"I'm on it."

Ordonez had a close call on the outer drive heading downtown. Two cop cars, lights flashing had just zipped past. The drive was crowded, or maybe they weren't as alert as they should have been. They may have been told his car would be more likely seen somewhere around the Ambassador hotel.

He had decided that spending the night in a dark alley near the OSON office wasn't a good move. He had to go to Constable. He wouldn't like the idea, but fuck it. The OSON boss was going to have a roommate. There was nowhere else to go. He had checked out of his hotel. He was going to kill Remeau in the park, get money from Constable, and drive home. The cops might be checking his night clerk and every other hotel or motel five miles from the Ambassador,

He left the drive for side streets and found parking in an alley in a neighborhood of apartment buildings, about a mile from the Ambassador. He pulled his lightweight suitcase from the trunk and began a walk that passed only two dog walkers until he reached Rush street, Lots of traffic there. Car and foot traffic. He walked among and past revelers until he turned onto the final two blocks to the hotel. Two feeble street lights barely lit the sidewalk. A pea soup mist had settled on the area..

He shivered in his pant and shirt outfit. There was a sweater in the suitcase but he didn't stop.

He decided to enter the hotel by the main entrance. He didn't want to be remembered by the bar crowd.

No doorman. Good. He entered the small empty lobby. The carpeting felt like a warm California beach. He was looking for and found a telephone alcove a few feet from the unmanned desk. A late evening operator asked how she could help.

He said, "Jeremiah Constable, please."

Constable might have been asleep. It wasn't his usual strong voice. "Hello."

Ordonez woke him up.

"It's me. I'm downstairs. What's your room number?"

Hesitation joined surprise, but the executive made a quick recovery. "Is this wise?"

Ordonez had heard of inactive late night operators who listened in. He was terse.

"Yes, vital importance."

Constable owed the Mexican. Was he in trouble? He thought he would hear from him from somewhere on the road with instructions where to send his fee.

He had to let him come up. If he said wait until morning the little man might bribe someone for his room number and pound on the door.

"All right,"

Constable , now completely awake, was confident he could deal with the man. Ordonez would want money and he could pay him now that he had no need to run himself. Ordonez hadn't been paid since the strike break. When it became necessary to kill Remeau it was as if the Mexican had become a high salaried employee.

Pay him twenty? His room had a wall safe not holding that much. There was enough cash in the office safe.

In his last call Ordonez told him Remeau had picked up the second Burnside payment. He thought Ordonez was lying, that he had gone piggish and had hijacked the cash. But if that had happened Ordonez might not be here.

Was he in danger from the Mexican? No. Ordonez valued him as an occasional employer. Blackmail? A Beachco agent found him once. Why would he risk a surprise bullet in the back of the head.

Ordonez came into the room smiling, holding out his hand.

"Thank you, Jeremiah. I had to come. The cops have an ident on my rental car, and they know it was driven by a Latin. The credit card I used will lead nowhere. The cops have to be checking all the hotels and motels. They could have found me sleeping in the car. I couldn't risk it."

 Constable said, "I understand. Sit down and relax. Let me get you a drink."

"Oh thanks. You won't have tequila.

Anything else will be fine."

Constable chuckled. He chose bourbon at the side board and poured three inches.

He said over his shoulder, "I am curious as to why you chose to go after Remeau and friend in a restaurant."

"A couple reasons. I'm not a gunman and I couldn't risk moving targets. I had to get close and I needed light. The big man tried to get his hands on me. He almost did."

He would not tell Constable that Remeau might still be alive.

"I got lucky when I saw Remeau leave the park. The son of a bitch got in and out of that toilet without me seeing him.

"I followed him on foot to their apartment building, but I had to go back for my car. When I came back they took off for a hotel. I don't know why, but I waited and followed them to the OSON meeting. The assholes for some reason wanted to hear Beach's pitch. But they saw you with me and that was a problem. I solved it by shooting them in the restaurant.

"I should get back to LA. I don't suppose you have much cash in the apartment, but tomorrow will be okay. I'll find a used car lot and get something that will get me across the country."

"Okay, sounds good, let's get some rest.

The couch should be comfortable for you. I'll get a blanket from the bedroom.

Constable had to plan his action for the next day. He had to assume the cops had a copy of the Remeau letter. It had to be on one of the dead men. He now wished he hadn't destroyed the damn thing. He was no lawyer, but the letter might not be enough for an arrest. It was signed by a "witness" who said he saw him with a Mexican strikebreaker in Kansas City.

It was too late to call Pam. She was with Beach in Detroit for a non-OSON meeting. He couldn't tell her about the letter, but he could cook up a reason for needing a lawyer.

If Carey just wanted an interview, ala his session with Beach, he could get by without a lawyer. With Remeau out of the picture what did Carey have?

He said, "All right. I'll get the cash from the office, first thing. Twenty should cover it."

Ordonez slammed his empty glass on the coffee table.

"Bullshit, man. I took care of two people who could put you in jail for the rest if your life, I can't risk trying to fly out. A goddamned car will cost at least ten. I need a lot more."

Constable stared. He had not poured himself a drink or he might have thrown it into the upturned face.

"I overpaid you and Remeau in Kansas City.

Twenty five and five more for getting it done fast, which was borderline. There was a fee for the outside legal talent, too."

Ordonez had twisted himself on the couch so that he was sitting on its edge. Constable, still standing, had an urge to run for the bathroom, lock himself in. He had given the angry man too much to drink. Was he going to pull his gun?

Ordonez shook his head. He had to calm down. Shoot the man? What the hell good would that do? Talking tough was a bad idea. Why make him mad enough to send someone after him in LA?

He forced a smile and sat back.

"Okay. I see where you're coming from. Give me twenty five."

Constable sat down. He held a look on the little man as if he was thinking it out.

"Okay, now let's get some sleep."

65

Remeau had a miserable night. The car's back seat made a rotten bed for a man of his bulk. The bullet in his side added to the discomfort.

It had turned cool and he started the car to flip on the heater. A breeze had come off Lake Michigan and blew off the mist but left a chill. He drove out of the alley and was an early customer at a McDonald's drive through. The black coffee and pair of sausage biscuits helped wake him up. He sipped and munched. And planned.

Clements wasn't sure the letter would work. As they drove to the Bear, he said, "It will shake the man up, but he's no dummy. With or without a lawyer he'll figure that without a name for the Mexican the letter doesn't prove a thing. What he doesn't want is for his boss to know, and he doesn't want cops and publicity that could hurt the OSON plan.

"He'll use the three days we gave him to send the Mexican after us, but where would he look? I'll get going on our passports tomorrow."

Clements was smart, but somehow the Mex found them. Jesus, seeing the poor guy go down like that was awful. He would find that little bastard. Mexicans didn't all look alike.

It didn't make a lot of difference to Ordonez but he wondered why Constable was in such a hurry. He slept well on the luxurious couch and could have used another hour.

Constable said, "We'll go in early just to make sure no one sees us together. You can wait in my car."

Constable used his phone for an early wake up call. Dressed, and fully awake he ordered a large breakfast from room service. For one. Ordonez shared the large serving of scrambled eggs and bacon and drank his coffee from a glass.

There was little conversation. A mutual wariness hung in the air. The relationship was not built on an expectation of friendship. They would not trade Christmas cards, and last night was a definite disconnect. Ordonez knew he would never again be called to do anything for Constable or Beachco.

Each man examined his priorities after their final separation. Constable had to minimize harm to OSON caused by possible police efforts to link him with the ballplayer's murder. Ordonez yearned for his beloved California and welcome arms from a petite woman who cooked wonderful Mexican meals.

Constable left the suite first. The car would be waiting in the garage for Ordonez who had changed his red shirt for one as black as his pants. He checked the Beretta automatic and filled the bullet clip. If cops showed up, he would not be dissed by a hand pushing his head through a police car door. No way was he spending the rest of his life in an American jail. It could not be.

No one was in the hall or elevator. Constable was parked on the third level. His Cadillac e was running and in gear.

66

Before dawn Remeau drove to a curb site close to the corner of Grand and Michigan, only a hundred feet from the OSON office. He would shoot Constable as the bastard entered the office. Before the cops could answer a 911 call he would be on a freeway a half mile up Grand. He would get off at the first exit, steal a car license, and get the hell out of Chicago using side streets. They might still probably get him, but not before he killed Constable.

The six-shot Colt was sitting in his lap. It was all he needed. but the pain in his side was getting worse. He had little sleep and felt faint. Jesus, he couldn't pass out.

He thought about Clements, sprawled on the Bear floor. Shit, he had grown to like the man. He didn't have much to do with him in school days, probably because Clements stayed out of trouble. Teachers liked him. He didn't seem to work at it, but he always had the right answers.

So why did he wind up crooked? He was smart enough to get jobs, but said he couldn't find anything that led to making some real money.

He said going to jail was the stupidest thing he ever did.

"For all practical purposes I was homeless. It was cold and I was desperate. I didn't have a gun, I just walked in that store, put a hand in my coat pocket and told the guy behind the counter to give me the money. He may have known a real crook from a phony. Whatever. He had a gun, and I was in the soup."

Schooling. Remeau conceded during the California days that getting more education was the answer to making money. He was lucky to hook on with the fire fighters, and he made a good move to learn bar tending. Punching out his boss was a mistake. He was half in the bag. At least he didn't get hooked on drugs.

He remembered the boredom of school. They shoved him along, couldn't dump him until he was eighteen. Jesus, he hated the women teachers the most. An ugly bunch of nags. They must have wished they could graduate him to a jail cell. The women he met since weren't much better. He only needed them for quick fucks. He paid when he had to, finally decided to head back to Chicago after hearing he was in trouble with the pimps. It was no one-on-one situation. They would have ganged up on him, or worse.

He did all right in Kansas City and the ball-player job seemed a piece of cake. It was too bad Burnside was so easy to cream. Clements held on too long.

He would be careful from here. He had some money and he could get more after he got that bullet out of his side. But he had to think more like Clements.

Hey, a new Cadillac was sliding into empty curb near the OSON door. Jesus, it was Constable leaving the car. He had guessed right. No cops waiting for Constable.. Not many people on the street. He struggled up and grabbed for the door handle.

Constable was looking for any sign of police presence as he neared the office. He knew he was being more than circumspect. Why would Carey for whatever reason come an hour before most offices in the area were open?

There. Only a couple of cars at the curb a few feet from the office. All the room in the world. He would be within a few strides of the office door.

"Sit tight Alex. I'll have your money in a couple of minutes. Then you can call a cab and be on your way. California, here you come."

Ordonez wasn't ready to make a friendly response.

He said, "If I can find a cheap car that will make it all the way."

Maybe he wouldn't have to, As they drove from the hotel he thought how he hated to waste money on a car for only one use.

Had the cops found his rental? If so they would have a couple cops in a unmarked car within a few yards. A cab would drop him off a few blocks away. He would use alleys to get close and wait, all night if necessary, If there watchers they would get relief sometime during the night. If no cops took over the watch there was no watch. He would be on a freeway in seconds. He could disguise the car someway, maybe a quick paint job. He could steal a license plate.

Shit. He was acting crazy. Buy a fucking car. He glanced at his watch. He would drive a thousand miles a day, maybe more. Sleep in the car. Hide in LA, enjoy the woman he loved. He had been away too long.

The distance between Remeau and his victim was less than twenty-five feet when a stunned Ordonez saw the huge man he thought he had killed stagger to the front of the Cadillac. He leaned on the hood in obvious agony, struggling to keep himself from falling.

"Noooo," Ordonez screamed as he wrenched his tiny gun from his pocket and clawed at the door handle.

Remeau was forced to hold up. He left his car hoping to close the distance between him and Constable in a few seconds. He wanted to yell for the man's attention, curse him, and make him turn and see that he was about to die

The pain ripping his body forced him into a limp across the street. The growing morning traffic screamed, tooted, and yelled. He stumbled against the Cadillac hood. He almost fell. He was going to have to shoot from much farther than he wanted, but he would fire every bullet.

He got off only one. Constable, door key in his hand, heard the explosion. When he saw its source, the man he thought dead, he sank to his knees, terrified.

The shot missed, and now Remeau was the target. He heard the yell from inside the car, but his only thought was to put bullets into Constable. Before he could pull the trigger again, he heard the Mexican's first shot, then no more as the rest of the slugs tore into his back. Ordonez from six feet, emptied the Beretta's clip into the man who had proved so hard to kill. His victim fell to his knees, then like a falling tree, toppled face first onto the concrete sidewalk.

The scene had witnesses, at least a dozen men and women, most of whom turned and ran. They included two female friends who fell into the arms of a pair of cops who had just left their favorite coffee and donuts shop a half block up Grand.

They had heard Ordonez's rapid fire. One of the officers used his shoulder phone to call for back up and an ambulance. His mate tried to calm the two female witnesses and learn what they had seen.

"Thank you ladies. Now please stay here."

Guns drawn the two intense men trotted down the sidewalk.

Constable saw Remeau go down. His terror was replaced by a fear of police. There were early morning people of the sidewalk. Someone would call 911. He held out the Cadillac keys to Ordonez . He couldn't be seen with the man,

"Take the car. Go"

Ordonez grabbed the keys. "Hell yes, but I want my money."

"It's a fifty thousand dollar car. Go, for Christ's sake. We can't be seen together."

Ordonez wanted to shoot the man. He would have, but a wisp of smoke was all that was left of his tiny gun's power to kill.

He glared at the frightened man he once viewed as a long term associate. He knew he had to run. He'd dump the car for whatever he could flush from a no-questions-asked used car hustler.

He spun away from Constable, but saw the two cops, guns pointing, weaving through morning traffic jam. More cops, sirens screaming, were rolling into the curb.

He wasn't going to get home, to beloved LA, its border of endless blue, its nights made joyful with always welcome tequila. And the woman with whom he would share the Kansas City bounty. It was sad. To the yells of "Police. Drop the gun," he aimed it at the nearest cop.

Leo and Bob Henry were driving west on 35th, just five miles north of the shooting. Leo was describing his disappointment over Judge Baldwin's telephone turn down.

"He remembered the Hodiak case, but the conviction had to withstand a couple of appeals. He said he needed more to think this one out.

Henry nodded in sympathy. He had invited Leo to join him for breakfast. Yesterday was brutal but it ended well. He was still exhausted from the search for the Mexican and wounded Remeau, but his wife, Helen, cheered him with the announcement his dollar in the state lottery had earned him fifty smackers. He wanted to treat.

Instead he heard a dispatcher crisply announce a shooting at Michigan and Grand.

Leo yelled, "It's near the OSON office. Let's go."

Henry spun the wheel for a one-eighty in front of a startled but fortunately alert eastbound driver and punched on the lights and siren.

At the sight of two men down, they witnessed another event adding to their city's swelling reputation as the murder capital of the United States. A Mayor who had tried to outlaw guns in his city was a loser to a militant National Rifle Association which was having its way in helping gun owners hold onto all forms of firearms.

The scene was crowded with pedestrians. Leo called out loudly, "Get back, people. Bob get me some breathing room."

He bent over the large man he knew had to be Remeau,

Hours later, he would philosophize with Henry, "Somewhere, somehow, this life turned sour. A wasted life. We've been involved with too many of them."

An ambulance was pulling up. Its crew was ready to do their thing, but Leo held them up.

"They are gone, fellahs. Cover them up and wait for the examiner."

He turned to the officers, who were not happy about shooting the little man. They would be made even more unhappy when they learned it was "death by suicide." The tiny empty automatic, often referred to as "Ladies aide," lay in the hand of its diminutive master.

Leo congratulated the officers. William O'Shaughnessy and Arthur Coulter.

"Good thing you guys were nearby. Maybe having coffee and in one of my favorite spots?"

He grinned and the men grinned back. Every cop in the city knew or heard of Leo Carey. Now they would do whatever he ordered.

He said, "See if you push these people away from the scene. Then you can go back on patrol or do paper work. Your choice. He nodded at the OSON door.

"Anyone in there?"

A male witness overheard Leo's question.

"The shooting began when a man was opening the office door. The large dead man shot at the man at the door. He was shot by the little man."

Leo thanked him and asked him to give his statement to Henry who was greeting the crime investigation crew.

How about this for a climax. A long tough trail might be coming to an end.

Someone had grabbed his elbow. It was Naomi Stafford. She was standing with one of her aides. She had not yet entered her office..

"Sergeant Carey, what has happened here?"

He looked down on the horrified young woman.

"We may have closure on the death of your friend, Clay Burnside."

Naomi asked, "What's it all about, Pam?"

"I only know Jeremiah is in trouble. I have to be with him and maybe find some criminal lawyer help. He said there was a shooting. Did you see anything?"

Naomi told her how she arrived right after two men were killed..

"Sergeant Carey had just arrived, too. He said. "We may have closure on Clay Burnside's murder."

Kirsten groaned, "Oh for Christ's sake."

She was gone for only an hour when two uniformed policemen came in, asking for her.

"Miss Stafford, we have a warrant to search the office of Jeremiah Constable."

They stayed for only a few minutes. Naomi didn't think they would find much. All OSON records were in her care, but they appeared satisfied and said thank you when they left.

Early that evening Leo sat in a Bear booth with, Henry, Sal and Sid Coffin. Corrine had served their drinks and pulled up a chair. It was a celebration, but not a noisy one.

Sid had welcomed Leo's call, but knew he didn't have a beat on the arrest.

"You'll announce this big event at a conference, but I'm still sitting pretty."

He nudged Leo. "I have the man who has the whooole story."

Leo took a sip of beer.

"Constable hired Alex Ordonez who recruited Remeau for the Beachco auto parts strike. Back in Chicago, Remeau was available for shutting up poor Clay Burnside. When Constable received the extortion letter he sent the Mexican to kill Remeau and his buddy."

Henry said, "How about Preston Beach and his OSON?"

Leo said, "I, you too, believed him when he said he had nothing to do with the murder, but to have his top man indicted is going to put a helluva shock to the movement. I'm pretty sure he is as stunned as anyone about Constable, but he is a man of incredible wealth, and he's young and looks to me as strong as a bull. He may carry on, but Constable is going to serve time. It's all in the hands of the lawyers now. And the DA is in very good shape."

Henry and Sid knew, but Sal said, "How?" followed by Corrine's, "Yeah, how?"

Leo had to smile.

"Mr. Constable kept up to date in erasing his cell phone messages with Alex Ordonez. We found the phone in his office. His expensive lawyers either failed to tell him the sim disk in his cell would also store his calls, or he just didn't get around to the task.

"We also have good news from Al Durkin at the Palmer House. One of his kitchen people will testify that one of the men who slipped through the hotel kitchen that terrible night was Mr. Remeau."

About the same time Naomi sat across from Brian Strang in a coffee shop on Grand.

"He said, "I'm done. Preston has asked me to replace Constable. Impossible. I'll stick around until his brain trust can come up with someone, but Jeremiah put his life into OSON. He just lost it when he thought Burnside was going to try to wreck everything for which he worked so hard."

She said, "I'm discouraged but not out. I will try to help Press. Whatever he's into. He may shift gears, possibly place OSON on hold, while he stumps for a better America. He may go political. He's a healthy, dynamic young man. If he sees improvement in the racial scene he may shelve OSON."

Brian smiled. "Naomi, you are very bright for a white girl. That little speech sums up things beautifully. I hope whatever happens won't send us on different paths."

Naomi thought she had fallen in love with Clay, but that could not be. Press said time heals all wounds. It wasn't an original thought, but like a lot of long-standing adages it stayed around because it was true. It looked as if Brian wanted to continue their friendship. Damn it. If he didn't she would.

In an exclusive interview with Sid Coffin, Preston Beach said, "Long before I began the collaboration with Jeremiah I thought the United States was in serious trouble. History has shown us time and again that when the wealth of a nation is held by a few to the extent this exists in the states there is an explosion.

"I liken our situation to that of Rome in the years centuries following Christ. There was the wealthy and there was the miserably poor and slavery. Our America has its own slavery. We call it 'Minimum wage."

"I'm among the super rich, but I'm still a young man. I want to do something more with excess cash than donate to dodge taxes. When Jeremiah told me he had access to all that African land in a temperate zone, the practicality of an OSON became possible."

Sid said, "And now?"

"OSON has taken a terrible hit, but the idea of a new nation created by people determined to follow the initial plan is still very much alive. We will be able to ship our first cadre surprisingly soon. You have our ten-year plan."

Sid said, "I told my friend, Leo Carey, that I think you have an underlying belief that OSON will help save our democracy."

"Yes, Sid, And I will make that claim at eve
I will challenge our politicians, and those who would aspire
public office, to dump the welfare system in exchange for a much stronger effort to bring Black America into our main society, usually known as the middle class. It can be done for a lot less than we are spending now,"

"How?

"Intensified education at the lower and high school levels, of course, especially with young children. Then we have to inspire and support more Black Americas to use the system that makes America what it is; that is, to create wealth. It begins with owning homes. Tragically, Black home ownership is at record lows. Black-owned businesses, always much smaller in proportion to White ownership aren't keeping up with population growth."

"You're implying that Black Americans are becoming a larger part of the overall population."

"More than implying, Yes, and OSON will leave America with even fewer Blacks who have entrepreneurial ambition. My hope is to see American leaders waking up to that problem and make a real effort to fix it."

Leo met with Leo and Marian over another of the lady's inspired dinners. Sid described his meeting with Beach over the pork tenderloin, confessing he wasn't sure how he would use Beach's words and opinion.

"But I'll definitely try to separate him from the terrible decision of his right-hand man. He's a hard guy not to like. And how often do you find an intellectual running a business empire and working on a project like OSON on the side?"

Leo agreed. "He's one of a kind, all right. I like him, too. It's a shame he has to be linked to a terrible crime."

"Yeah. A crime that will be linked with the Chicago White Sox scandal of a century ago. Now Marian, I could use a little more gravy."

William L. "Bill" Prentiss, a Chicagoan, is a
graduate of the University of Illinois and a veteran
of WW II. He was a staff writer with the Associated
Press before a forty-year career in advertising and
public relations. He began writing novels and
non-fiction after retirement. CHICAGO COPS APB
was inspired by the senseless murders of
huge numbers of young African-American men and
women. Mr. Prentiss lives in Clearwater, FL